The Curlytops Snowed In

Howard Roger Garis

The CURLYTOPS SNOWED IN

HOWARD R. GARIS

TED'S SLED WAS RUNNING AWAY, AND DOWN THE
DANGEROUS SLOPE.

THE CURLYTOPS
SNOWED IN
OR
Grand Fun with Skates and Sleds

BY

HOWARD R. GARIS
AUTHOR OF "THE CURLYTOPS SERIES," "BEDTIME
STORIES," "UNCLE WIGGILY SERIES," ETC.

Illustrations by
JULIA GREENE

NEW YORK
CUPPLES & LEON COMPANY

1941

THE CURLYTOPS SERIES

By HOWARD R. GARIS

12mo. Cloth. Illustrated.

THE CURLYTOPS AT CHERRY FARM Or, *Vacation Days in the Country*

THE CURLYTOPS ON STAR ISLAND Or, *Camping Out With Grandpa*

THE CURLYTOPS SNOWED IN Or, *Grand Fun With Skates and Sleds*

THE CURLYTOPS AT UNCLE FRANK'S RANCH Or, *Little Folks on Ponyback*

CUPPLES & LEON COMPANY, New York

CONTENTS

CHAPTER

CHAPTER I
A LETTER FROM GRANDPA

"TED! Teddy! Look, it's snowing!"

"Oh, is it? Let me see, Mother!"

Theodore Martin, who was seldom called anything but Teddy or Ted, hurried away from the side of his mother, who was straightening his tie in readiness for school. He ran to the window through which his sister Janet, or Jan as she liked to be called, was looking.

"Oh, it really is snowing!" cried Ted in delight. "Now we can have some fun!"

"And look at the big flakes!" went on Jan. "They're just like feathers sifting down. It'll be a great big snowstorm, and we can go sleigh-riding."

"And skating, too!" added Ted, his nose pressed flat against the window pane.

"You can't skate when there's snow on the pond," objected Jan. "Anyhow it hasn't frozen ice yet. Has it, Mother?"

"No, I think it hasn't been quite cold enough for that," answered Mrs. Martin.

"But it'll be a big snowstorm, won't it?" asked Jan. "There'll be a lot of big drifts, and we can wear our rubber boots and make snowballs! Oh, what fun, Ted!" and she danced up and down.

"And we can make a snow man, too," went on Teddy. "And a big snowball!"

"An' I frow snowballs at snow man!" exclaimed the voice of a smaller boy, who was eating a rather late breakfast at the dining-room table.

"Oh, Trouble, we'll make you a little snow house!" cried Jan, as she ran over to his high chair to give him a hug and a kiss. "We'll make you a snow house and you can play in it."

"Maybe it'll fall down on him and we'll have to dig him out, like the lollypop-man dug Nicknack, our goat, out of the sand hole when we were camping with grandpa," added Ted with a laugh. "Say, but it's going to be a big storm! Guess I'd better wear my rubber boots; hadn't I, Mother?"

"I hardly think so, Teddy," said Mrs. Martin. "I don't believe the snow will get very deep."

"Oh, Mother, won't it?" begged Jan, as if her mother could make it deep or not, just as she liked.

"Why won't it be a big storm, Mother?" asked Teddy. "See what big flakes are coming down," and he looked up at the sky, pressing his face hard against the window. "Why won't it?"

"Because it seldom snows long when the flakes are so big. The big flakes show that the weather is hardly cold enough to freeze the water from the clouds, which would be rain only it is hardly warm enough for that. It is just cold enough now to make a little snow, with very large flakes, and I think it will soon turn to rain. So you had better wear your rubbers to school and take an umbrella. And, Teddy, be sure to wait for Janet on coming home. Remember you're a year older than she is, and you must look after her."

"I will," promised Teddy. "If I have to stay in, Jan, you wait for me out in front."

"Will you have to stay in, Teddy?"

"I don't know. Maybe not. But our teacher is a crank about things sometimes."

"Oh, The-o-dore Mar-tin!" exclaimed his mother, speaking his name very slowly, as she always did when she was displeased or was quite serious, "you must not say such things about your teacher."

"Well, the other boys say she's cranky."

"Never mind what the other boys say, you must not call her that. Teachers have it hard enough, trying to see that you children know your lessons, without being called cranks. Don't do it again!"

"I won't," promised Teddy, just a bit ashamed of himself.

"And get ready to go to school," went on his mother. "Did you clean your teeth—each of you—and comb your hair?"

"I did," said Janet.

"I cleaned my teeth," announced Ted, "but my hair doesn't need combing. I combed it last night."

For most boys this would hardly have been of any use, but with Teddy Martin it was different. Teddy's hair was so curly that it was hard work to pull a comb through it, even though he went slowly, and when he had finished it was curlier than before, only more fluffed up. Janet's was the same, except that hers was now getting longer than her brother's.

No wonder then that the two children were called "Curlytops;" for their hair was a mass of tangled and twisted ringlets which clung tightly to their heads. Everyone called them Curlytops, or just Curlytop, of course, if one happened to meet Teddy or Janet alone.

"I think you'd better give your hair a little brushing this morning, anyhow, Teddy," his mother said. "You can get a few of the wrinkles out."

"Well, if I do they won't stay," he answered. "Oh, but look at it snow!" he cried. "The flakes are getting smaller; don't you think so, Jan?"

"I think so—a little."

"Then it'll last and be a big storm, won't it, Mother?" he asked anxiously.

"Well, maybe so. But you don't want too big a storm, do you?"

"I want one big enough for us to go coasting on the hill and have sleigh-rides. And we can skate, too, if the pond freezes and we scrape off the snow. Oh, we'll have fun, won't we, Jan?"

Without waiting for an answer Ted ran upstairs to take a few of the "wrinkles" out of his curly locks, while Nora Jones, who helped Mrs. Martin with the housework, looked for the children's umbrella and rubbers.

It was the first snowstorm of the season, and, as it always did, it caused much delight, not only to the Curlytops but to the other children of Cresco where the Martin family lived. Janet watched eagerly the falling flakes as she put on her rubbers and waited for Teddy to come down from the bathroom, where he had gone to comb his hair, though he could not see much use in doing that.

"It'll only be all curly again," he said. But still he minded his mother.

"The flakes are getting lots smaller," said Janet, as she and Teddy started for school. "We'll have big heaps of snow, Ted, and we can have fun."

"Yes, I think it will be more of a storm than I thought it would amount to at first," said Mrs. Martin. "I'm glad we have plenty of coal in the cellar, and an abundance of dry wood. Winter has started in early this year."

"And pretty soon it'll be Thanksgiving and Christmas!" cried Ted. "Then what fun we'll have!" exclaimed the excited boy.

"Now don't get any snow down inside your collars," called Mrs. Martin to her children, as they went down the street.

"We won't!" they promised, and then they forgot all about it, and began snowballing one another with what little snow they could scrape up from the ground, which was now white with the newly-fallen crystals.

"I'm going to wash your face!" suddenly cried Ted to his sister.

"You are not!" she cried, and away she ran.

Meanwhile, Trouble Martin, which was the pet name for Baby William, the youngest of the family, sat in the dining-room window and laughed at the falling flakes and at his brother and sister going to school, romping on their way.

"There, I did wash your face!" cried Ted, as he finally managed to rub a little snow on his sister's cheek, making it all the redder. "I washed your face first this year!"

"I don't care. You got some down inside my collar and my neck's wet and I'm going to tell mother on you!"

"Oh, don't!" begged Ted. "I won't do it again, and I'll wipe your neck with my handkerchief."

"Well, maybe I won't tell if you don't do it again," promised Janet, while her brother got out his pocket handkerchief.

"Ouch! Oh!" cried Janet, as Teddy started to dry her neck. "Your handkerchief's all wet! It's got a lot of snow on it! Let me alone!" and she pushed him away.

"Wet? My handkerchief wet?" asked Ted. "So it is!" he exclaimed. "I guess some snow must have got in my pocket. I'll use yours, Jan."

"No, I don't want you to. I'll wipe my own neck. You let me alone!"

Jan was laughing; she did not really care that Ted had washed her face, and she soon had her neck quite dry. Then the two Curlytops hurried on to school.

The street was filled with children now, all going to the same place. Some paused to make a slide on the sidewalk, and others took turns running and then gliding along the slippery place.

"Oh, here's a dandy one!" called Tommie Wilson, who lived not far from Teddy Martin. The two boys saw a long smooth place on the sidewalk in front of them, where some early school children had made a slide.

"Come on!" cried Tommie, taking a run.

"Come on!" yelled Teddy.

One before the other they went down the sidewalk slide.

"Look out for me!" called Janet and she, too, took a running start.

But alas for the children. Near the end of the slide one of Tommie's feet slid the wrong way and after he had tried, by waving his arms, to keep upright, down he went in a heap.

"Get out the way!" cried Teddy. But Tommie had no time, and right into him slid Ted, falling down on top of his chum, while Jan, not able to stop, crashed into her brother and then sat down on the slide with a bump. All three were in a heap.

"Oh, Tommie Wilson!" cried Janet, looking at her books which had fallen out of her strap. "See what you did!"

"I couldn't help it!"

"You could so! You tripped on purpose to make me fall!"

"I did not, Janet Martin."

"No, it wasn't Tommie's fault," declared Teddy. "He couldn't help it. Are you hurt Jan?"

"No—not much—but look at my books."

"I'll pick 'em up for you," offered Tommie, and he did, brushing off the snow. Then he helped Janet to get up, and she began to laugh. After all it was only fun to fall on a slippery slide.

"There goes the bell!" cried Teddy, when he had helped brush the snow off his sister's skirt.

"One more slide!" exclaimed Tommie.

"I'm going to have one, too!" called Teddy.

"You'll be late for school, and be kept in!" warned Janet.

"We'll run," Tommie said, as he started at the top of the slippery place.

He and Ted had their one-more slide, and then, taking hold of Janet's hands, they hurried on to school.

Behind them and in front of them were other children, some hurrying to their classes, others waiting for a last slide, some falling down in the snow. Others were washing one another's faces and some were snowballing.

In school the teachers had hard work to keep the minds of their pupils on their lessons. Every now and then some boy or girl would look out of the window when his eyes ought to have been on spelling book or geography. All wanted to see the snow sifting down from the clouds.

The flakes, that had been large at first, were now smaller, and this, as most of the children had been told, meant that the storm would last. And they were glad, for to them snow meant grand winter fun with sleds and skates.

"We'll have some bobsled races all right," whispered Teddy Martin to Tommie Wilson, and the teacher, hearing what Teddy said, kept him after school for whispering. But she did not keep him very long, for she knew what it meant to have fun in the first snow of the season.

Teddy found Janet waiting for him when he came out, for it was now snowing hard and Teddy had taken the umbrella with him when he went to his room. He was a year older than his sister and one class ahead of her in school.

"Were you bad in class?" Janet asked.

"I only whispered a little. She didn't keep me in long. Come on now, we'll have some fun."

And fun the Curlytops and their playmates did have on their way home from school. They slid, they snowballed, they washed one another's faces and some of the boys even started to roll big snowballs, but the flakes were too dry to stick well, and they soon gave this up. It needs a wet snow to make a big ball.

When Teddy and Janet got home, their cheeks red, their eyes sparkling and their hair curlier than ever because some snow had gotten in it, they found their mother reading a letter which the postman had just left.

"Oh, what's it about?" asked Jan. "It's from Cherry Farm, isn't it, Mother? I can tell by the funny black mark on the stamp."

"Is it from grandpa?" asked Teddy.

"Yes," answered Mrs. Martin. "The letter is from grandpa."

"Is he coming here to spend Christmas, or are we going there just as you said we might?" asked Janet.

"I'm not sure about either one yet," replied her mother. "But grandpa sends his love, and he also sends a bit of news."

"What is it?" asked Ted.

"Grandpa Martin writes that an old hermit, who lives in a lonely log cabin in the woods back of Cherry Farm, says this is going to be the worst winter in many years. There will be big snowstorms, the hermit says, and Grandpa Martin adds that the hermit is a good weather prophet. That is, he seems to know what is going to happen."

"A big snowstorm! That will be fun!" cried Teddy.

"Maybe not, if it is too big, "warned his mother. "Grandpa Martin says we ought to put away an abundance of coal and plenty of things to eat."

"Why?" asked Janet.

"Because we may be snowed in," answered her mother.

CHAPTER II
A RUNAWAY SLED

FOR a moment Ted and Janet looked at their mother. Sometimes she told them strange things, and she did it with such a serious face that they could not always tell whether or not she was in earnest.

"Do you mean that the snow will come up over the top of the house so we can't go out?" asked Teddy.

He remembered a picture his mother had once showed him of a lonely log cabin in the woods, almost hidden under a big white drift, and beneath the picture were the words: "Snowed in."

"If it comes up over the top of the house we can't ever get out till it melts," went on Jan. "Will it happen that way, Mother? What fun!"

"Dandy!" cried Ted.

"Oh, indeed! Being snowed in isn't such fun as you may think," said Mrs. Martin, and then the Curlytops knew their mother was now a little bit in earnest at least.

"Of course," she went on, "the snow will hardly cover our house, as it is much larger than the one in the picture I showed Teddy. But being snowed in means that so much snow falls that the roads are covered, and the piles, or drifts, of the white flakes may be high enough to come over the lower doors and windows.

"When so much snow falls it is hard to get out. Even automobiles and horses can not go along the roads, and it is then people are 'snowed in.' They can not get out to buy things to eat, and unless they have plenty in the house they may go hungry.

"That is what Grandpa Martin meant when he said we might be snowed in, and why he warned us to get in a quantity of food to eat."

"But shall we really be snowed in, Mother?" asked Ted.

"I don't know, I'm sure. Grandpa was only telling us what the hermit told him. Sometimes those old men who live in the woods and know much about nature's secrets that other persons do not know, can foretell the weather. And the snow has certainly come earlier this year than for a long time back. I am afraid we shall have a hard winter, though whether or not we shall be snowed in I cannot say."

"Well, if we're going to be snowed in let's go coasting now, Janet!" suggested Ted to his sister.

"May we, Mother?" asked the little girl.

"Yes. But don't go on the big hill."

"No. We'll stay on the small one."

Teddy ran out of the room to get the sled.

"Me want to go on sled!" cried Baby William.

"Oh, Trouble! We can't take you!" said Jan.

"I wish you could," said Mrs. Martin. "He hasn't been out much to-day, and I want to get him used to the cold weather. It will be good for him. He loves the snow. Just give him a little ride and bring him back."

"All right," agreed Janet. "Come on, Trouble. I'll help you get your cap and jacket on."

"Is he comin' with us?" demanded Ted, as he got his sled and Janet's down out of the attic, where they had been stored all summer. "I'm not goin' coasting with him!"

"Don't forget your 'g's,' Teddy," said his mother gently.

"Well, I don't want to take the baby coasting," and Teddy was careful, this time, not to drop the last letter as he sometimes did from words where it belonged. "Can't have any fun with him along!"

"I'll just give him a little ride," whispered Janet. "You boys will have to make the hill smooth anyhow, and we girls can't have any fun till you do that. So I'll ride Trouble up and down the street for a while."

"Oh, all right. And I'll take him coasting some other time," promised Ted, a little bit ashamed of the fuss he had made. "We'll go on and get the hill worn down nice and smooth."

It was still snowing, but not very hard, and the ground was now two or three inches deep with the white flakes—enough to make good coasting when it had been packed down smooth and hard on the hill which was not far from the home of the Curlytops. There were two hills, the larger, long one being farther away.

At first the runners of the two sleds were rusty, but Ted scraped them with a piece of stone and they were soon worn smooth and shiny so they would glide along easily.

Trouble was delighted at the chance of being taken out on his sister's sled. Janet gave her little brother a nice ride up and down the sidewalk, and then she ran and rode him swiftly to the house where her mother took him up the steps. Trouble did not want to go in, and cried a little, but his mother talked and laughed at him so that he soon smiled. Mrs. Martin wanted Janet to have some fun with Teddy on the hill.

There were a number of boys and girls coasting when Janet reached the place where her brother had gone. The hill had now been worn smooth and the sleds shot swiftly down the hill.

"Come on, Janet!" cried her brother. "It's lots of fun! I'll give you a push!"

Janet sat on her sled at the top of the hill, and Ted, with a little running start, thrust her along the slope. Down went Janet, the wind whistling in her ears.

"Look out the way! Here I come, too!" cried Ted behind her. "I'll race you to the bottom!"

But Janet had a good start and Ted could not catch up to her, though he did beat Tommie Wilson who had started at the same time the Curlytop lad had.

With shouts and laughter the children coasted on the hill. At the bottom they came to a stop on a level place, though some of the older boys gave their sleds an extra push and then went on down another hilly street that was a continuation of the first. At the foot of this street ran the railroad and there was some danger that sleds going down the second hill might cross the tracks. Of course, if there were no trains this would have been all right. But one could never be certain when a train would come, so most of the children were told never to go down the second hill. They could not do it unless they pushed their sleds on purpose, over the level place at the bottom of the first hill.

"I wouldn't want to ride down there," said Teddy, as he saw some of the larger boys fasten their sleds together in a sort of "bob," and go down the second hill together.

"No, this little hill is good enough," Janet replied.

She and Teddy, with their boy and girl friends had great sport coasting on the snow. It was getting dusk, and some of the smaller children had gone home.

"We'd better go, too," said Janet. "It's snowing again, Ted, and maybe it will happen—what grandpa's letter said—we'll be snowed in."

"Well, I'm going to have one more coast," Teddy answered.

"I'll wait for you," returned his sister.

She saw her brother slide down the small hill and come to a stop on the level place at the bottom. Then, before Ted could get off his sled, down came a lot of the big boys, riding together on a bob.

"Look out the way!" they called to Teddy. "Look out the way! We're going fast and we can't stop! We're going down the second hill! Look out the way! Clear the track!"

But Teddy had no time to get out of the way. In another second, before he could get up off his sled, the bob of the big boys crashed into him and sent him over the level place and down the second hill.

Ted's sled was really running away with him, and down the dangerous slope.

"Oh, Teddy! Teddy!" cried Janet when she saw what had happened. "Come back! Come back!"

But Teddy could not come back. His sled was a runaway and could not be stopped. Luckily Teddy had not been hurt when the big boys ran into him, and he managed to stay on his sled. But he was going very fast down the second hill.

"Oh, dear!" cried Janet, and down she ran after her brother.

I will take just a moment here to tell my new readers a little about the Curlytops, so they may feel better acquainted with them. Those who have read the first volume of this series may skip this part. That book is entitled "The Curlytops at Cherry Farm," and tells of Janet and Ted's summer vacation, which was spent at the home of Grandpa Martin. They found a stray goat, which they named Nicknack, and they had many good times with their pet. They also met a boy named Hal Chester, who was being cured of lameness at a Home for Crippled Children, not far from grandpa's house. Grandpa Martin had on his farm many cherry trees and how the "lollypop" man helped turn the cherries into candy is told in the book.

The second volume is called "The Curlytops on Star Island," and relates the experiences of the two children, with Trouble and their mother, when camping with grandpa on an island in Clover Lake. On the island Ted and Janet saw a strange blue fire, though they did not learn what caused it until after they had met a strange "tramp-man" who sometimes stayed in a cave.

When their camping days on Star Island came to an end, the Curlytops went back to their home in the town of Cresco, where Mr. Martin owned a large store. And now we find them coasting down hill.

As for the children themselves, you have already been told their names. Theodore and Janet they were, but more often they were called just Ted and Jan. Baby William was generally called "Trouble," because he got in so much of it. But Mother Martin usually called him "dear Trouble." He often went with Jan and Ted when they rode with Nicknack, and Trouble had adventures of his own. Besides Mr. and Mrs. Martin there was Nora, the maid.

Grandpa Martin has been mentioned, and of course there was Grandma Martin. They lived at Cherry Farm. Mrs. Martin's sister, Miss Josephine Miller, lived in the city of Clayton.

Aunt Jo, as the children called her, owned, besides her city home, a country place in Mt. Hope on Ruby Lake. She said she would some day build a nice, new bungalow at the lake.

Another relative, of whom the Curlytops were fond, was Uncle Frank Barton. He was really Mr. Martin's uncle, but Ted and Jan claimed him as their own. He had a big ranch near Rockville, Montana, and the children hoped to go there some day.

Besides their goat, Ted and Jan had a dog named Skyrocket and a cat called Turnover, because she would lie down and roll over to get something to eat. The dog's name was given him because he was always so lively, running and jumping here, there and everywhere.

And now that you have learned more about the family, you will, perhaps, wish to hear what was happening to Teddy.

Down the second hill he went on his runaway sled, very fast, for the bob of the big boys had struck his coaster quite a blow. And the second hill was much more slippery than the first, some of the boys having sprinkled it with water, that had frozen into ice.

"Oh, dear!" thought poor Ted, as he went sliding down faster and faster. "I'm afraid!"

And well he might be, for at the foot of the hill, where the railroad crossed, he could now hear the puffing of an engine and the ringing of a bell.

"Ted! Teddy! Come back! Stop!" cried Jan, as she ran down the hill. But Teddy could neither stop nor come back just then.

CHAPTER III
NICKNACK ON THE ICE

JANET MARTIN did not know what to do. In fact, a girl much older than Ted's sister would have been puzzled to know how to stop the little boy on his runaway sled from going across the railroad tracks. Of course he might get across before the train came, but there was danger.

"Oh, dear!" cried Jan. "Those big boys were mean to bunk into Ted, and push him over the second hill!"

She was tired now, and running down a slippery hill is not easy. So Jan stood still. Many of the other coasters did not know that Ted was in danger. They saw the larger boys coasting down the second hill, and perhaps they thought Teddy knew what he was about as long as his sled was going so straight down the same slope.

For Ted was steering very straight. With his feet dangling over the back of his sled he guided it down the hill, out of the way of other boys, some of whom he passed, for his sled was a fast one.

Teddy was frightened. But he was a brave little fellow, and some time before he had learned to steer a sled with his feet, so he was not as afraid as he might otherwise have been.

"Oh, what will happen to him?" wailed Janet, and tears came into her eyes. As soon as she had shed them she was sorry, for it is not very comfortable to cry wet, watery, salty tears in freezing weather.

"What is the matter, Curlytop?" asked a bigger girl of Jan. This girl had been giving her little brother and sister a ride on her sled.

"My brother is sliding down the second hill, and there's a train coming," sobbed Jan. "He'll be hurt! We never go on that hill!"

The big girl looked down at Ted. He was quite far away now, but he could easily be seen.

"Maybe he'll stop in time," said the big girl. "Oh, look!" she cried suddenly. "He's steered into a snow bank and upset!"

And this was just what Ted had done. Whether he did it by accident, or on purpose, Jan could not tell. But she was still afraid.

"He'll get hurt!" she said to the big girl.

"Oh, I guess not," was the answer. "The snow is soft and your brother would rather run into that, I think, than into a train of cars. Come on, I'll go down the hill with you and see if he is all right. You stay here, Mary and John," she said to her little brother and sister, placing them, with their sled, where they would be out of the way of the other coasters.

"I'll leave my sled here, too," said Jan, as she went down the hill with the older girl.

When they reached Teddy he was brushing off the snow with which he had become covered when he slid, head first, into the drift alongside the road.

"Are you hurt?" cried Jan, even before she reached him.

"Nope!" laughed Ted. "I'm all right, but I was scared. I thought I'd run over the track. Those fellows nearly did," and he pointed to the boys on the bobsled, which they had made by joining together two or three of their bigger sleds, tying them with ropes, and holding them together as they went down hill by their arms and legs.

The boys on this bobsled had stopped just before going over the track when the switchman at the crossing had lowered the gates. He was now telling the boys they must not coast down as far as this any more, as trains were coming. And, as he spoke, one rumbled by.

"You might have been hurt by that if you had not stopped your sled in time," said the big girl to Ted.

"That's what I thought," he answered. "That's why I steered into the snow bank."

"Those big boys were mean to shove you down the second hill," declared Janet.

"Well, maybe they didn't mean it," said the big girl.

"No, we didn't," put in one of the larger boys, coming up just then. "We're sorry if we hurt you, Curlytop," he added to Ted.

"You didn't hurt me, but you scared me," was the small boy's answer.

"You certainly know how to steer," said the bigger boy. "I watched you as we passed you on the hill. I knew if we got to the bottom first we could keep you from getting hurt by the train. Now you and your sisters sit on my big sled, and we'll pull you to the top of the hill to pay for the trouble we made."

"I'm not his sister," said the big girl.

"I am!" exclaimed Jan quickly.

"I might have known that. You two have hair just alike, as curly as a carpenter's shaving!" laughed the big boy. "Well, hop on the sled, and you, too," he added, nodding at the big girl. "I guess we can pull you all up."

"Course we can!" cried another big boy, and when Ted, Jan and the larger girl, whose name was Helen Dolan, got on the largest of the sleds that had made up the bob, they were pulled up the two hills by a crowd of laughing boys, Teddy's sled trailing on behind.

So the little incident did not really amount to much, though at one time both Ted and Jan were frightened. They coasted some more, being careful to keep out of the way of the bigger boys and girls and then, as it was getting dark, Jan said again they had better go home.

"One more coast!" cried Ted, just as he had said before. "It may rain in the night and melt all the snow."

"It's awful cold," shivered Janet, buttoning up her coat. "If it tries to rain it will freeze into snow. And it's snowing yet, Ted."

"Yes. And almost as hard as it was this morning. Say, maybe we'll be snowed in, Jan! Wouldn't it be fun?"

"Maybe. I never was snowed in; were you?"

"No. But I'd like to be."

The time was to come, though, when Ted and Janet were to find that to be snowed in was not quite so much fun as they expected.

They reached home with rosy cheeks and sparkling eyes, to find supper ready for them.

"Did you have a good time?" asked their mother.

"Fine!" answered Janet.

"And I got run away with," added Ted, who always told everything that happened.

"Run away with!" exclaimed his father. "I thought they didn't allow any horses or automobiles on the coasting hill."

"They don't," Ted answered. "My sled ran away with me, but I steered it into a snow bank and upset," and he told of what had happened.

"You must be very careful," said his father, when Ted had finished. "Coasting is fun, but if everyone is not careful you may get hurt, and we wouldn't like that."

It was still snowing hard when Ted and Jan went to bed, and it was with eager faces that they looked out into the night.

"Do you s'pose we'll be snowed in?" asked Jan.

"I hope so—that is, if we have enough to eat," answered Ted. "That's what grandpa said to do—buy lots to eat, 'cause the hermit said it was going to be an awful bad winter."

"Did you ever see a hermit, Ted?"

"No. Did you?"

"No. But I'd like to, wouldn't you?"

"Yes, I would, Jan."

"Maybe I'll be a hermit some day," went on the little girl, after she had gotten into bed, her room being across the hall from Ted's.

"Huh! You can't be a hermit."

"I can so!"

"You can not!"

"Why?"

"'Cause hermits is only men. I'll be the hermit!"

"Well, couldn't I live with you—wherever you live?"

"Maybe I might live in a dark cave. Lots of hermits do."

"I wouldn't be afraid in the dark if you were there, Teddy."

"All right. Maybe I'd let you live with me."

"Does a hermit like snowstorms, Teddy?"

"Children, you must be quiet and go to sleep!" called Mrs. Martin from downstairs. "Don't talk any more."

Ted and Janet were quiet for a little while, and then Janet called in a loud whisper:

"Teddy, when you're a hermit will you have to eat?"

"I guess so, Jan. Everybody has to eat."

"Children!" warned Mrs. Martin again, and then Jan and Ted became quiet for the rest of the night.

It was very cold when the children awoke in the morning, and as soon as they were up they ran to the windows to look out. It had stopped snowing and the air was clear and bright with sunshine.

"We didn't get snowed in," called Janet, in some disappointment.

"No," answered Ted. "But it's so cold I guess the pond is frozen and we can go skating."

"Oh, that'll be fun!" cried Jan. "Will you help me skate, Ted? 'Cause I can't do it very well yet." She had just learned the winter before.

"I'll help you," her brother promised.

There was a pond not far from the Martin home, and it was so shallow that it froze more quickly than the larger lake, which was just outside the town, and where the best skating was. The smaller boys and girls used the little pond, though sometimes they went to the lake when it was perfectly safe.

After school Jan and Ted, taking their skates, went to the pond. There they found many of their little friends.

"How's the ice?" asked Teddy of Harry Kent.

"Slippery as glass," was the answer.

"Then I'll fall down!" exclaimed Jan.

And she did, almost as soon as she stood up on her skates. But Ted and Harry held her between them and before long she could strike out a little. Then she remembered some of the directions her father had given her when he taught her to skate the year before, and Jan was soon doing fairly well. Ted was a pretty good skater for a boy of his age.

"You're doing fine, Curlytop!" called Harry Morris, one of the big boys who had pulled Ted and Jan up the hill on his sled the previous night. He had come to see how thick the ice was. "You're doing fine. But why don't you hitch up your goat and make him pull you on the ice?"

"Oh, Ted, we could do that!" cried Janet, as the big boy passed on.

"Do what?"

"Harness Nicknack to a sled and make him give us a ride. Maybe he could pull us over the snow as well as on the ice."

"We'll try it!" cried Teddy.

He took off his skates and hurried home, telling Janet to wait for him at the pond, which was not far from the Martin house. In a little while Teddy came back driving Nicknack hitched to Ted's sled. The goat pulled the little boy along over the snow much more easily than he had hauled the small wagon.

"This is great!" cried Ted. "I'm going to drive him on the ice now. Giddap, Nicknack!"

Teddy guided the goat to the ice-covered pond. Nicknack took two or three steps on the slippery place and then he suddenly fell down, the sled, with Ted on it, gliding over his hind legs.

"Baa-a-a-a!" bleated Nicknack, as if he did not at all like this.

CHAPTER IV
THE SNOW HOUSE

"OH, Teddy, you'll hurt Nicknack!" cried Janet, when she saw what had happened.

"I didn't mean to," Ted answered, jumping off the sled. "He slipped on the ice and I couldn't stop the sled."

"Help him get up," went on Jan. "He can't get up himself with that sled on his hind legs."

Teddy pulled back the sled, but still Nicknack did not get up.

"Maybe one of his legs is broken," suggested Tom Taylor, a boy who lived near the Martins.

"If it is he'll have to run on three legs. Our dog did that once, when one of his legs had been run over," said Lola Taylor, Tom's sister.

"Come on, Nicknack, get up!" cried Ted. "Stand up and give us a ride on the ice."

But the goat only went: "Baa-a-a-a!" again, and he seemed to shake his head as if to say that he could not get up.

"His legs are all right," Teddy said when he had looked at them as well as he could, and felt of the parts that stuck out from under Nicknack's body. "Why doesn't he stand up?"

"What's the matter, Curlytop?" asked Harry Morris.

"My goat won't stand up on the ice," Ted answered. "He fell down and his legs are all right, but he won't stand up."

"Maybe it's because he knows he can't," said Harry. "Goats aren't made to stand on slippery ice you know. Their hoofs are hard like a cow's. They are all right for walking on snow or on the ground, but they can't get a good hold on the ice. I guess the reason Nicknack won't stand up is because he knows he'd fall down again if he tried it. Here, I'll help you get him over into the snow, and there you'll see he'll be all right."

With the help of Harry, the goat was half led and half carried off the pond to the snow-covered ground. There Nicknack could drag the sled easily, and he gave Ted and Jan a nice ride, also pulling Lola and Tom.

Ted offered the big boy a ride behind the goat, but Harry said:

"I'm much obliged to you, Curlytop, but I'm afraid your sled is too small for me. Your goat is strong enough to pull me, I guess, but I'd fall off the sled, I'm afraid."

"I wish I could make him pull me on the ice," said Teddy. "How could we make him stop slipping?" he asked the big boy.

"Well, you'd have to have sharp-pointed iron shoes put on his hoofs, the same as they shoe horses for the winter. Only I don't know any blacksmith that could make shoes small enough for a goat. Maybe you could tie cloth on his hoofs, or old pieces of rubber, so he wouldn't slip on the ice."

"That's what we'll do!" cried Teddy. "To-morrow we'll make some rubbers for our goat, Jan."

"Do you think he'll let us put 'em on?" asked Jan.

"Oh, course he will. Nicknack is a good goat."

Ted and Jan drove him around some more in the snow, and this was not hard pulling for Nicknack, as the sled slipped along easily and he had no trouble in standing up on his sharp hoofs in the soft snow. But Ted did not again drive him on the ice that day.

"I know what we can do to have some fun," said Jan, as she and her brother started Nicknack toward home after having had some more rides themselves, and giving some to their little friends.

"What?" asked Ted. "Haven't we had fun enough?"

"Yes, but we can have more," went on Jan. "And this fun is good to eat."

"If you mean stopping at a store and getting some lollypops—nopy!" and Ted shook his head quickly from side to side.

"I didn't mean that," declared Jan.

"It's good you didn't," came from her brother, "'cause if you did we couldn't."

"Why not?" Jan asked.

"I haven't got a penny," returned Teddy. "I asked mother for some when I went home to get Nicknack, but she told me to wait a minute while she paid the milkman."

"Didn't you wait?" asked Jan in some surprise. It seemed strange that Teddy would miss a chance like this, as Mrs. Martin did not give the Curlytops pennies every time they asked for them. She did not want them to get in the habit of spending money too freely, especially when it was given them, and they had done no little thing to earn it. Nor did she want them to buy candy when she did not know about it. So the giving of pennies was really an event in the lives of Ted and Jan, and the little girl wondered very much now, why it was her brother had not taken the money when his mother was willing to give it.

"Why didn't you want to wait, Ted?" asked Jan.

"Oh, I wanted to all right," he answered; "but Nicknack didn't want to. I got him—Nora and me—all harnessed up, and I tied him out in front; then I went in to ask for the pennies—one for you and one for me."

"Oh, I wish you'd got 'em," said Jan, rather sorrowfully.

"I would have, only for the goat," explained her brother. "Mother told me to wait; but, just as she said it, I saw an automobile come along in front of our house close to where I'd tied Nicknack.

"Our goat got scared and tried to run away, 'cause the auto chucked snow on him, and then I had to run out to catch him. That's why I couldn't wait for the pennies. I jumped on the sled just as Nicknack was startin' to run away — —"

"Star-ting!" corrected Janet.

"Well, star-ting, then," laughed Ted. "Anyhow, I couldn't make him turn around to go back for the pennies, so I came on right over to the pond."

"And we had a lot of fun there," stated Jan. "Only I didn't like to see our goat fall down."

"Well, he'll stand up when we get rubbers for him," said Ted. "But how're we going to have more fun, Jan?"

"Make snow-cream," answered the little Curlytop girl.

"What's that?" asked Ted. "Like ice-cream?"

"Yes, only different. Don't you know? Mother lets us make it sometimes. You take a lot of snow—clean snow in a pail—and you stir some eggs and milk and sugar and flavoring in it, and that makes almost the same as ice-cream."

"How're we going to do it?" asked Ted, as the goat pulled him and his sister slowly along the snow-lined street. "We haven't got any sugar or milk or eggs or flavoring—not even a pail."

"We can stop at Aunt Sallie's and get 'em all," said Janet. "She'll like us to make snow-cream, I guess. She can help us eat it."

"Then let's!" cried Teddy. "Go on, Nicknack, we're going to make snow-cream! Is it awful good?" he asked his sister.

"Terrible good," she answered. "I didn't have any yet this winter, but we had some last. It's better'n lollypops."

"Then it must be specially extra good," decided Ted. "Hurry up, Nicknack."

The goat hurried as much as he could, but, though it was easier going on the snow than on the ice, still it was not as easy as on the dry ground in summer.

Along the street, around this corner, then around the next went the Curlytops on the sled pulled by Nicknack, until, at last, they came to the house of Aunt Sallie, a dear old lady who was always glad to see them.

"My gracious sakes alive!" she cried, as she met the two children. "Here we come, in our coach and four, just like Cinderella out of the pumpkin pie!"

"Oh, Cinderella didn't come out of a pumpkin *pie*, Aunt Sallie!" gasped Janet.

"No? Well, I was thinking of some pumpkin pies I just baked, I guess," said Aunt Sallie Newton, who was really Mrs. Martin's aunt, and so, of course, the Curlytops' great-aunt, though they called her "Aunt" Sallie, and not "Great-aunt" Sallie. "Yes, I guess that was it — the pumpkin pies I baked. Maybe you'd like some?" she asked, looking at the children.

"Oh, I just guess we would!" cried Teddy eagerly.

"And we'd like some snow-cream, too, if you please," said Jan. "Could we make some, Aunt Sallie?"

"Snow-cream?"

"Yes, like mother used to make. You take some snow," went on the little girl, "and stir it up with milk and sugar and eggs — —"

"Oh, yes! I know!" laughed Aunt Sallie. "I used to make that when I was a little girl. Now I'll tell you what I'll do; if you're sure it will be all right with your mother, I'll get you each a little piece of pumpkin pie and then I'll make the snow-cream."

"Oh, goodie!" cried Jan and Teddy exactly together.

So, while Nicknack stayed outside in a sheltered corner by the house and nibbled the dried leaves of some old flowers, Aunt Sallie got the

26

pieces of pie for the children, each slice on a nice little plate with a napkin under it.

"And now for the snow-cream!" said Aunt Sallie.

She went out into the kitchen, and almost before Jan and Ted had finished their pieces of pie back she came with two dishes with something good in them.

"I made it just as you told me," she said to Jan. "I stirred the eggs and sugar and milk up in some clean snow and flavored it. Tell me if you like it."

The children tasted, and Ted exclaimed:

"I could eat three dishes!"

"But I guess one will be enough after the pie," said Aunt Sallie, and Ted thought so, too, after he had finished the nice dessert. Then he and his sister, after thanking Mrs. Newton, went out and got on the sled again, hurrying Nicknack on, for it was growing late. They were soon safe at their own home.

"Mother, are there any old rubbers in the house?" asked Ted that night, after having told of the fun skating on the pond and riding over the snow behind Nicknack.

"Old rubbers? What do you want of them?" asked Mrs. Martin.

"I want to make some overshoes for the goat."

"Overshoes for the goat! What will you try next, Teddy?" and his mother laughed.

"We really are going to do it," added Jan. "Nicknack can't stand up on the slippery ice without something on his hoofs."

"Why don't you get him a pair of skates?" asked Father Martin with a laugh. "Though you'd have to get him two pairs, to have enough to go around, as Nicknack has four feet."

"He couldn't stand up on skates," answered Ted. "His hoofs are like skates now, they're so hard and shiny."

"And so you think overshoes would be the thing?" asked his father. "Well, maybe they would do. I'll see if I can find some old rubbers or rubber boots that you can cut up."

A pair of boots that had holes in them and could no longer be used by Mr. Martin, were found in the attic. Some pieces of rubber were cut from the legs and when the inside lining had been partly peeled off four thin squares of rubber could be cut out.

"We'll tie these on Nicknack's hoofs and see if he can stand up on the ice," said Teddy. "I wish it was to-morrow now, so we could do it."

Ted and Jan hurried home from school the next day to hitch Nicknack to Ted's sled and drive him down to the ice to try the goat's new rubbers. They were tied on his hoofs with pieces of string, Mrs. Martin helping the children do this. Nicknack was a gentle and patient goat, but he acted rather strangely when the rubber squares were tied over his hoofs.

He stamped his feet, shook his head and bleated. He did not quite understand what was going on, but he made no special trouble and started off well when he had been hitched to the sled.

"Me want a wide!" called Trouble from the veranda, as Ted and Jan went gliding away over the snow.

"Next time!" answered Ted.

"This sled isn't big enough," added Janet. "We ought to get a bigger sled, Teddy," she went on. "One as big as our goat wagon, and then we could have fine rides and take Trouble with us."

"We'll ask daddy to get us one," said her brother.

When they reached the pond the only skaters on it were Tom and Lola Taylor. Tom laughed as he saw Nicknack.

"Ho!" he cried, "your goat will fall down on the ice again."

"Maybe he won't," answered Teddy. "Just you watch!"

He drove Nicknack toward the frozen pond, but the goat stood still at the very edge.

"He's afraid to go on—he knows he'll slip," said Tom.

"I guess that's it," agreed Teddy. "Go on, Nicknack!" he called. "Giddap! You won't fall 'cause you've your rubbers on."

"Oh! has he, really?" asked Lola.

"'Deed he has. We made him some out of an old rubber boot," replied Teddy. "Look!" and he pointed to the black squares tied on Nicknack's hoofs.

"How funny!" gasped Lola.

"Maybe he won't slip with them on," remarked Tom, "but I guess he isn't sure of it. He won't go on the ice."

And indeed Nicknack did not seem to want to do this. He turned first to one side and then the other as Ted tried to drive him on to the frozen pond. Nicknack did not mind pulling the Curlytops over the snow, where he knew he would not slip, but he was afraid of the ice.

"I know how to get him on," said Teddy.

"How?" asked Tom.

"Here, you hold this cookie in front of him," went on Teddy. "I put it in my pocket to eat myself, but I'll give it to Nicknack. Hold it in front of his nose, Tom, and when he goes to bite it you just walk away with it. Then he'll follow after you, and when you walk on the ice he'll do the same."

"Say, that is a good way!" cried Tom. "I'll do it!"

"Once he's on the ice, if the rubbers keep him from slipping, he'll be all right," went on Ted.

He tossed Tom the cookie and Tom held it in front of the goat's nose. Surely enough Nicknack reached out for it, but as soon as he did this Tom stepped back a little way, the goat following.

29

This was done two or three times, Nicknack getting nearer the icy pond each time, until at last he had all four rubber-covered feet on it.

"Shall I give him the cookie now?" asked Tom.

"No, make him come a little farther for it," answered Ted, who was sitting on the sled in front, holding Nicknack's reins, while Janet sat behind her brother.

So Tom backed a little farther away from the goat, that still walked on to get the cookie which he could smell, and which he wanted very much. And before Nicknack knew it he was walking over the ice and he did not slip at all, for the pieces of rubber on his hoofs held him up, just as they would have held up Teddy or Janet.

"Now he's all right!" called Teddy. "He can walk on the ice now, and run, too, I guess. Give him the cookie, Tom."

So Nicknack had the cookie, and then Teddy drove him over and around the pond. Nicknack seemed to like it, now that he did not slip.

When Teddy and Janet had had a good ride they let Tom and Lola take a turn, Tom driving, and the goat went as well for him as it had gone for Teddy.

"I didn't know a goat was as much fun in winter as it is in summer," said Tom. "I wish I had one."

"We'll give you more rides when we get a big sled," promised Ted.

"Are you going to get one?" Lola asked.

"We're going to ask our father for one," replied Ted. "And I guess he'll let us have it so we can take Trouble out for rides. Giddap, Nicknack!" and once more he started the goat across the ice.

The Curlytops and their friends had great sport with the goat and sled that day, and Nicknack hardly slipped at all. He was getting used to the ice, Tom said.

After two days during which the Curlytops had fun with their sleds and skates, it began to snow again, covering the ground yet deeper with the white flakes, while the frozen pond and lake were buried out of sight.

"No more skating for a while," said Tom Taylor, as he walked to school with Teddy and Jan one morning.

"No. But we can sleigh-ride and build a snow fort," answered Ted.

"And a snow man, too," added Janet.

"Why not make a snow house?" asked Lola. "The snow is soft and it will pack well. Let's make a snow house!"

"We will!" cried Ted. "We'll start one after school in our back yard. We'll make one big enough for us all four to live in."

"And we can stay there even if the snow covers the top," added Janet.

"Wouldn't we freeze?" asked Lola.

"No. Mother read us a story about a man who was caught out in a big snowstorm, and he dug down under the snow and let it cover him all up, except a place to breathe, and he was warm."

"Well, we'll build a snow house, but I guess there won't be enough snow to cover it," cried Tom.

"I like lots of snow," put in Teddy.

All that day it snowed, even when the Curlytops and the other children ran laughing and shouting out of school. Tom and Lola went with Jan and Ted to the Martins' back yard and there they began to build a snow house.

CHAPTER V
NICKNACK SEES HIMSELF

THE snow was just right for making snow houses, or for rolling big balls that grow in size the more you push them along. For the snow was wet—that is, the flakes stuck together. Sometimes, when the weather is cold, the snow is dry and almost like sand. Then is not a good time to try to make snow houses, snow men or big snowballs.

"But it's just right now!" cried Teddy, as he ran into the back yard with his sister and the other girl and boy. "We'll make a fine snow house!"

"First we'll make some big snowballs," said Tom Taylor.

"I thought we were going to make a snow house!" exclaimed Ted.

"So we are," agreed Tom. "But the way to start is to make big snowballs. Roll them as big as you can and they'll make the sides of the house. We'll pile a lot of snowballs together and fill in the cracks between. That's the way to start."

Ted and the others saw that this was a good way, and so they began. First they each made a little snowball. But as they rolled them along around the big yard the balls gathered the snow up from the ground, packing it around the little ball that had first been started, until Ted's was so big that he could hardly move it.

"It's big enough now!" called Tom. "Put it over here, where we're going to start the snow house, and I'll roll my big ball next to yours, Ted."

This was done. Then Jan's snowball, and that of Lola were put in a row and the four walls of the snow house were started. There was plenty of the snow to be had and the children worked fast. Before dusk they had the four walls of the house made, with a doorway and windows cut, but there was no roof on, though the walls of the white house were above Tom's head, and he was the tallest.

"FIRST WE'LL MAKE SOME BIG SNOWBALLS," SAID TOM
TAYLOR.

"Aren't we going to make a roof?" asked Ted.

"We'll do that to-morrow," answered Tom. "We ought to have some
boards to lay across the top, and then we could pile snow on them.
It's easier that way, but you can make a roof of just snow. Only it
might fall in on our heads."

"We don't want that," said Janet. "Boards are better, Tom."

When it was too dark to see to do any more work on the snow building, the Curlytops went into the house and their playmates hurried to their home for supper.

"We'll finish the house to-morrow," called Teddy to Tom.

The next afternoon, when they came home from school, the children started to make the roof. Ted had asked his father to get him some boards, and this Mr. Martin had done. They were laid across the top of the four walls, and snow was piled on top of them, so that from the outside the house looked as if made entirely of snow. From the inside the boards in the roof showed, of course, but no one minded that.

The snow house was large enough for five small children to get in it and stand up, though Tom's head nearly touched the roof.

"But that doesn't count," laughed Ted. "You can pretend you're a giant and you could lift the roof off with your head if you wanted to."

"Only you mustn't want to!" cautioned Jan.

"I won't," promised Tom.

"We ought to have a door so we could close it, and then it would be like a real house," Lola said.

"Couldn't we make one?" asked Ted.

"It would be hard to make a door fast to the snow sides of the house," answered Tom. "If we had a blanket we could hang it up for a curtain-door, though."

"I'll get one!" cried Janet, and she ran in to ask her mother for one.

The blanket was tacked to the edge of one of the boards in the roof, and hung down over the square that was cut out in the snow wall for the door. When the blanket was pulled over the opening it was as cozy inside the snow house as one could wish.

"And it's warm, too!" cried Ted. "I guess we could sleep here all night."

"But I'm not going to!" exclaimed Jan quickly. "Anyhow we haven't got anything to sleep on."

"We can make some benches of snow," Tom said. "Let's do it!"

"How?" asked Ted.

"Well, we'll just bring in some snow and pile it up on the floor along the inside walls. Then we can cut it square and level on top, as high as we want it, and we can sit on it or lie down on it and make-believe go to sleep."

"That'll be fun!" cried Lola.

With their shovels the Curlytops and the others were soon piling snow up around the inside walls of the white house. Then the benches were cut into shape, and they did make good places to sit on; though it was too cold to lie down, Mrs. Martin said when she came out to look at the playhouse, and she warned the children not to do this.

"We ought to have a chimney on the house," suggested Tom, after he had gone outside to see how it looked.

"We can't build a fire, can we?" asked Jan, somewhat surprised.

"No, of course not!" laughed Ted. "A fire would melt the snow. But we can make a chimney and pretend there's smoke coming out of it."

"Let's do it!" cried Lola.

"All right," agreed Tom. "You're the lightest, Teddy, so you get up on the roof. You won't cave it in. I'll toss you up some snow and you can make it square, in the shape of a chimney."

This Ted did, and with a stick he even marked lines on the snow chimney to make it look as if made of bricks.

"That's fine!" cried Tom. "It looks real!"

"It would look realer if we had something like black smoke coming out," declared Janet.

"Oh, I know how to do that!" exclaimed Lola.

"How?" asked her brother.

"Get some black paper and stick it on top of the chimney."

"Maybe my mother's got some," said Ted. "I'll go and ask her."

Mrs. Martin found an old piece of wrapping paper that was almost black in color, and when this had been rumpled up and put on top of the snow chimney, where Ted fastened it with sticks, at a distance it did look as though black smoke were pouring out of the white snow house.

"Now we ought to have something to eat, and we could pretend we really lived in here," said Janet, after a bit, when they were sitting on the benches inside the house.

"You go and ask mother for something," suggested Ted. "I got the paper smoke. You go and get some cookies."

"I will," Janet promised, and she soon came running from the house with a large plate full of molasses and sugar cookies that Nora had given her.

"Um! but these are good!" cried Tom, as he munched some with the Curlytops and his sister.

"This is a fine house!" exclaimed Teddy. "I'm glad you helped us build it," he said to Tom.

"Only it wants some glass in the windows," said Ted, looking at the holes in the snow walls of the house.

"We don't need glass," immediately put in Tom.

"Why not?" asked Jan. "If we put wooden windows in we can't see through 'em."

"We can use sheets of ice!" cried Tom. "My father said that that's the way the Eskimos do up at the north pole. They use ice for glass."

"You can see through ice all right," said Ted. "But where could we get any thin enough for windows for our snow house?"

"All the ice on the pond and lake is covered with snow," added Lola.

"We can put some water out in pans," went on Tom. "If it's cold to-night it will freeze in a thin sheet of ice, and then to-morrow we can make windows of it for our snow house."

"Oh, that'll be fun!" cried Ted.

"It will be almost like a real house!" added Jan.

Mrs. Martin said, when the Curlytops asked her, that Tom's plan might work if the night turned cold enough to freeze. And as after dark it did get colder she put some water out in large shallow pans. In the morning the water was frozen into thin sheets of ice, clear as crystal, and Ted and Jan could see right through them as well as they could see through glass.

"They're great!" cried Tom when he saw them, and that afternoon when school was out, the ice windows were set in the holes in the walls of the snow house.

"'Dis nice place!" Trouble said, when he was taken out to it. "I 'ikes it here! I stay all night!"

"No, I guess you won't stay all night," laughed Tom. "You might freeze fast to the snow bench."

"How plain we can see out of the windows," said Lola. "Oh, see, Ted, here comes your goat! I guess he's looking for you."

"He must 've got loose and 've run out of his stable," said Teddy. "I'll go to fasten him up. Here, Nicknack!" he called as he walked out of the snow house toward his pet.

Nicknack kept on coming toward the white house. He walked up to one of the windows. The sun was shining on it and as Ted looked he cried:

"Oh, I can see Nicknack in the glass window just as if it was a looking glass. And Nicknack can see himself!"

This was true. The goat came to a sudden stop and looked at his own reflection in the shiny ice window. Nicknack seemed much surprised. He stamped in the snow with his black hoofs, and then he raised himself up in the air on his hind feet. At the same time he went:

"Baa-a-a-a! Baa-a-a-a-a!"

"Oh, Nicknack's going to buck!" cried Ted.

"Who's he going to buck?" asked Tom, sticking his head out of the blanket door of the snow house.

"I guess he thinks he sees another goat in the shiny ice window," went on Ted, "and he's going for that. Oh, look out! Come back, Nicknack! Come back!" Teddy yelled.

But with another bleat and a shake of his head Nicknack, having seen himself reflected in the ice window, and thinking it another goat, started on a run for the snow house, inside of which were Jan, Tom, Lola and Trouble.

CHAPTER VI
THE SNOW MAN

SOUNDING his funny, bleating cry, like a sheep, Nicknack gave a jump straight for the ice window in which he had seen himself as in a looking glass.

"Crash!" went the ice window.

"Oh, my!" screamed Lola, inside the snow house.

"What is it?" asked Jan, for Lola stood in front of her.

Trouble looked up from where he was sitting beside Tom on the snow bench, and just then the goat went right through the soft, snow side of the house and scrambled down inside.

"Dat's our goat!" exclaimed Trouble, as if that was the way Nicknack always came in. "Dat's our goat!"

For a moment Jan and Lola had been so frightened that they did not know what it was. Luckily they were not in Nicknack's way when he jumped through, so he did not land on them.

But the snow house was so small that there was hardly room for a big goat inside it, besides the four children, even with Ted outside, and Nicknack almost landed in the laps of Tom and Trouble when he jumped through. In fact, his chin-whiskers were in Trouble's face, and Baby William laughed and began pulling them as he very often did.

"Baa-a-a-a!" bleated the goat and then he quickly turned around to see, I suppose, what had become of the other goat against which he had leaped, intending to butt him out of the way.

"Oh, Nicknack!" cried Jan. "What made you jump in on us like that?"

"Oh, my, I'm so scared!" gasped Lola. "Will he bite us?"

"Nicknack never bites," answered Janet reprovingly. "But what made him jump into the snow house and break the ice window?"

"'Cause he saw himself in it," answered Ted, coming in just then. "I knew what he was goin' to do but I couldn't stop him. Say, Tom, he made an awful big jump!"

"I should say he did!" exclaimed Tom. "I thought the whole place was coming down! You'd better call your goat out, Curlytop, or he may knock our snow house all to pieces."

"All right, I will," agreed Ted. "Here, Nicknack!" he called. "Come on outside!"

Nicknack turned at the sound of his little master's voice, and just then he saw another ice window. The sun was shining on that, too, and once more Nicknack noticed the reflection of himself in the bright ice, which was like glass.

"Baa-a-a-a!" he bleated again. "Baa-a-a-a!"

"Look out! He's going to jump!" cried Tom.

He made a grab for the goat, but only managed to get hold of his short, stubby tail. To this Tom held as tightly as he could, but Nicknack was not going to be stopped for a little thing like that.

Forward he jumped, but he did not quite reach the ice window. Instead his horns and head butted against the side wall of the snow house, and in it he made a great hole, near the window.

This made the wall so weak that the snow house began to cave in, for the other wall had almost all been knocked down when the goat jumped through that.

"Look out!" cried Ted. "It's going to fall!"

"Come on!" yelled Tom, letting go of Nicknack's tail.

"Take care of Trouble!" begged Jan of her brother.

Ted caught his little brother up in his arms. It was as much as he could do, but, somehow or other, Ted felt very strong just then. He was afraid Trouble would be hurt.

And then, just as the children hurried out of the door, pulling away, in their haste, the blanket that was over the opening, the snow house toppled down, some of the boards in the roof breaking.

"Oh, it's a good thing we weren't in there when it fell!" cried Lola. "We'd all have been killed!"

"Snow won't kill you!" said her brother.

"But the boards might have hurt us," said Lola. "Our nice house is all spoiled!"

"And Nicknack is under the snow in there!" cried Ted.

"No, he isn't! Here he comes out," answered Janet. And just as she said that, out from under the pile of boards and the snow that was scattered over them, came Nicknack. With a wiggle of his head and horns, and a scramble of his feet, which did not have any rubber on now, Nicknack managed to get out from under the fallen playhouse, and with a leap he stood beside the children.

"There, Nicknack! See what you did!" cried Janet.

"Spoiled our nice snow house!" added Lola.

"We'll build you another," promised Ted. "Say, I never knew our goat was such a good jumper."

"He's strong all right," agreed Tom.

"Nicknack a funny goat!" laughed Trouble, as his brother set him down on a smooth place in the snow.

"I guess Trouble thinks it was all just for fun," said Tom. "He isn't scared a bit."

"Oh, Trouble doesn't get scared very easy," answered Jan. "He's always laughing. Aren't you, Trouble?" and she hugged him.

"Well, shall we build the house over again?" asked Tom, when Ted had taken the goat back to the stable and fastened him in so he could not easily get loose.

41

"It'll be a lot of work," said Lola. "You'll have to make a whole new one."

"Yes, Nicknack didn't leave much of it," agreed Tom. "Shall we make a bigger one, Ted—big enough for Nicknack to get in without breaking the walls?"

"Oh, I don't know," returned Ted slowly. "There isn't much snow left, and some of the boards are busted. Let's make a snow man instead."

"All right!" agreed Tom. "We'll do that! We'll make a big one."

"I don't want to do that," said Jan. "Come on, Lola, let's go coasting."

"An' take me!" begged Trouble.

"Yes, take him," added Ted. "He'll throw snowballs at the snow men we make if you don't."

So Baby William was led away by the two girls, and Tom and his chum started to make a snow man. But they soon found that the snow was not right for packing. It was too hard and not wet enough.

"It's too cold, I guess," observed Tom, when he had tried several times to roll a big ball as the start in making a snow man.

"Then let's us go coasting, too," proposed Ted, and Tom was willing.

So the boys, leaving the ruins of the snow house, and not even starting to make the snow man, went to coast with the girls, who were having a good time on the hill with many of their friends.

"Oh, it's snowing again!" cried Ted when the time came to go home, as it was getting dusk.

"We've had a lot of storms already this winter," added Lola.

"My grandpa wrote in a letter that a hermit, up near Cherry Farm, said this was going to be a bad winter for storms," put in Jan. "Maybe we'll all be snowed in."

"That'll be great!" cried Tom.

"It will not!" exclaimed his sister. "We might all freeze to death. I don't like too much snow."

"I do!" declared Ted. "And there's a lot coming down now!"

There seemed to be, for the white flakes made a cloud as they blew here and there on the north wind, and it was quite cold when the Curlytops and their friends reached their homes.

All the next day it snowed, and Ted and Jan asked their father and mother several times whether or not they were going to be snowed in.

"Oh, I guess not this time," answered Mr. Martin. "It takes a regular blizzard to do that, and we don't often get blizzards here."

Though they felt that possibly being snowed in might not be altogether nice, still Ted and Jan rather wanted it to happen so they could see what it was like. But that was not to come with this storm.

Still the wind and snow were so bad, at times, that Mrs. Martin thought it best for the Curlytops to stay in the house. Trouble, of course, had to stay in also, and he did not like that a bit. Neither did Jan or Ted, but there was no help for it.

"What can we do to have some fun?" asked Teddy, for perhaps the tenth time that day. He stood with his nose pressed flat against the window, looking out at the swirling flakes. "Can't I be out, Mother?" he asked again.

"Oh, no, indeed, little Curlytop son," she answered.

"But we want some fun!" chimed in Jan. "Isn't there *anything* we can do?"

"Have you played with all your games?" asked her mother.

"Every one," answered the little girl.

"And we even played some of 'em backwards, so's to make 'em seem different," put in Teddy.

"Well, if you had to do that it must be pretty hard!" laughed Mrs. Martin. "I know it isn't any fun to stay in the house, but to-morrow the storm may be over and then you can go out. I know that won't help matters now," she went on, as she saw that Teddy was about to say something. "But if you'll let me think a minute maybe I can plan out some new games for you to play."

"Oh, Mother, if you only can!" cried Jan eagerly.

"Don't talk—let her think!" ordered Teddy. "We want to have some fun—a lot of fun!"

So he and his sister sat very quietly while his mother thought of all the things that might be possible for a little boy and girl and their baby brother to do when they had to stay in the house.

"I have it!" cried Mrs. Martin at last.

"Something for us to play?" asked Janet.

"Yes. How would you like to play steamboat and travel to different countries?"

"Not real?" cried Ted, with a look at the snow outside.

"Oh, no, not *real*, of course," said his mother, with a smile. "But you can go up in the attic, and take the old easy chair that isn't any good for sitting in any more. You can turn that over on the floor and make believe it's a steamboat. In that you and Jan and Baby William can pretend to travel to different countries. You can say the floor is the ocean and you can take some blocks of wood to make the islands, and if any one steps in the make-believe water he'll get his feet wet."

"Make-believe wet," laughed Teddy.

"That's it," his mother agreed with a laugh. "Now run along up and play, and then you won't think about the snow and the storm. And before you know it—why, it will be night and time to go to bed and in the morning the storm may be over and you can be out."

"Come on!" cried Jan to her brother.

44

"Wait a minute," he said, standing still in the middle of the room, while Trouble, who seemed to know that something was going on different from usual, jumped up and down, crying:

"We hab some fun! We hab some fun!"

"But you mustn't jump like that up in the attic," said his mother, shaking her finger at him. "If you do you'll rattle the boards and maybe make the plaster fall."

"Do you mean the plaster like the kind I had on when I was sick?" asked Jan.

"No, my dear, I mean the plaster on the ceiling," said her mother. "Well, Teddy, why don't you go along and play the game I told you about?" she asked, as she saw the little boy still standing in the middle of the sitting-room. "Play the steamboat game with the old chair. The chair will be the ship, and you can take the old spinning wheel to steer with, and maybe there's a piece of stovepipe up there that you can use for a smokestack. Only, for mercy's sake, don't get all black, and don't let Trouble get black."

"Come on, Ted!" cried his sister to him.

"I was just thinkin'," he said thoughtfully. "Say, Mother, don't folks get hungry when they're on a ship?"

"I guess so, Ted."

"And even on a make-believe one?"

"Well, yes, I suppose they do. But you can make believe eat if you get make-believe hungry."

"But what if we get *really* hungry?" asked Teddy. "I'm that way now, almost. Couldn't we have something real to eat on the make-believe steamboat, Mother?"

Mrs. Martin laughed.

"Why, yes, I suppose you could," she answered. "You children go on up to the attic and get the old chair ready to play steamboat, and I'll see what I can find to bring up to you to eat."

"Now we can have some fun!" cried Ted, and he no longer looked out of the window at the snow, and wished he could be in it playing, even though that was not exactly good for him.

Up the stairs trooped the Curlytops, followed by Trouble, who grunted and puffed as he made his way, holding to the hem of Jan's dress.

"What's the matter, Trouble?" asked Jan, turning around.

"Maybe he's making believe he's climbing a mountain," said Ted. "You always have to breathe hard when you do that."

"Did you ever climb a mountain?"

"No, but I ran up a hill once," answered her brother, "and that made my breath come as fast as anything. I guess that's what Trouble is doing."

"No, I is *not*!" exclaimed the little boy, who heard what his sister and brother were saying about him. "I 'ist is swimmin', like I did at Cherry Farm," he said. "I play I is in the water."

"I guess he's ready to play steamboat, all right," laughed Jan. "Come along, little fat Trouble!" she called, and she helped him get up the last of the steps that led to the attic.

The children found an old easy chair. It was one Mr. Martin had made some years before, and was a folding one. It had a large frame, and could be made higher and lower by putting a cross bar of wood in some niches. The seat of the chair was made of a strip of carpet, but this had, long ago, worn to rags and the chair had been put in the attic until some one should find time to mend it. But this time never seemed to come.

Often, before, Ted, Jan and Trouble had played steamboat with it. They laid it down flat, and then raised up the front legs and the frame part that fitted into the back legs. These two parts they tied together and could move it back and forth, while they made believe the carpet part of the chair was the deck of the boat.

"All aboard!" called Janet, as Teddy laid the chair down on the floor.

"Wait a minute!" called her brother.

"What for?" Janet wanted to know.

"'Cause I haven't got the steerin' wheel fixed. I got to get that, else the boat will go the wrong way. Wait until I get the old spinning wheel for a steerer."

Up in the attic, among many other things, was an old spinning wheel, that used to belong to Mrs. Martin's mother's mother—that is the great-grandmother of the Curlytops. The spinning part of the wheel had been broken long before, but the wheel itself would go around and it would make something to steer with, just as on the real large steamers, Ted thought.

The spinning wheel was put in front of the chair steamboat, and then Jan got on "board," as it is called.

"Wait for me!" cried Trouble, who was hunting in a corner of the attic for something with which to have some fun.

"Oh, I won't forget you," laughed Jan, and then all three of the children were ready for the trip across the make-believe ocean.

They crowded together on the carpet deck of the chair boat while Ted twirled the wheel and Jan moved the legs back and forth as if they were the engine. Trouble cried "Toot! Toot!" he being the whistle, and they rode about—at least they pretended they did—and had lots of fun, stopping at wooden islands to pick cocoanuts and oranges from make-believe trees.

"Here comes mother with something real to eat!" cried Teddy, after a bit, and up to the attic did come Mrs. Martin with some molasses cookies. The children had lots of fun eating these and playing, and before they knew it, night had come, bringing supper and bedtime.

Toward evening of the second day it stopped snowing, and the next day was quite warm, so that when Ted and Jan went out to play a bit in the snow before going to school, Ted found that the white flakes would make fine snowballs.

"Oh, it packs dandy!" he cried. "We can make the snow man this afternoon!" and he threw a snowball at Nicknack's stable, hitting the side of it with a bang.

"Yes, this will make a good snow man," said Tom after school, when he and Ted tried rolling the large balls. "We'll make a regular giant!"

And they started at it, first rolling a big ball which was to be the body of the snow man.

CHAPTER VII
A STRANGE BEDFELLOW

AROUND and around in the back yard, near what had once been a snow house, but which was only a big drift now, went Ted and Tom, rolling balls to make the snow man. Finally Ted's ball was so large that he could not push it any more.

"What'll I do?" he asked Tom. "Shall I leave it here and make the snow man right in this place?"

"No. I'll help you push it," Tom said. "We want that for the bottom part of the snow man, so it will have to be the biggest ball. Wait, I'll help."

The two boys managed to roll the ball a little farther, and it kept getting larger all the while, for as it rolled more snow clung to it and was packed on.

"There, I guess it's big enough," panted Tom, after a while. "Now, we'll pile my ball on top and then we'll put a head on our man."

"Where's his legs goin' to be?" asked Jan, who came out of the house just then to look on for a while, bringing Trouble with her.

"Oh, we'll carve them out of the lower part of the big snowball," answered Ted. "I'll show you."

With a shovel he and Tom cut away some of the snow, making big, fat, round, white legs for the man, who, as yet, had neither eyes, a nose nor a mouth, to say nothing of ears.

"Now we've got to have some buttons for his coat and some eyes for his head," said Tom, when the legs were made. On them the snow man stood up very straight and stiff.

"What do you want for eyes?" asked Ted.

"I saw a snow man in Grace Turner's yard last year," said Jan, "and that one had pieces of coal for eyes."

"That's just what we'll use!" cried Tom.

"I'll get the coal in our cellar," offered Ted, as he ran away to get the black lumps.

"Bring a lot and we'll make some buttons for his coat," called Tom.

"I will," Ted answered.

"Don't get the lumps too big!" shouted Jan.

"No, I won't," replied Ted; then he ran on to do his errand.

Two of the largest chunks of coal were stuck in the snow head of the man, and now he really began to look like something. The rest of the coal was stuck in the larger snowball and the black lumps looked just like coat buttons in two rows.

"There's his nose!" exclaimed Tom, as he fastened a lump of snow in the middle of the man's fat face. "And here's his mouth," he went on as he made a sort of cut in the snow with a stick.

"Oh, that doesn't look like a mouth," cried Janet. "I know a better way than that."

"Pooh! girls don't know how to make snow men!" exclaimed Ted. "You'd better go and get your doll, Janet."

"I do so know how to make a snow man, Theodore Martin! And if you think I don't I won't tell you the best way to make a mouth! So there!" and Janet, with her head held high in the air, and her nose up-tilted, started away, taking Trouble with her.

"Oh, I didn't mean anything!" protested Ted. "I was only foolin', Jan!"

"That's right!" added Tom. "Go on, tell us how to make a good mouth. Mine doesn't look much like one, but that's the way I always make 'em when I build a snow man."

"Well, I'll tell you," said Jan, turning back. "You want to take a piece of red flannel or red paper. Then it looks just like the snow man had red lips and was stickin' out his red tongue. I mean sticking," she added, as she remembered to put on her "g."

"Say! that *is* a good way to make a mouth, Ted!" cried Tom. "We'll do it. But where'll we get the red flannel?"

"I've got a piece of red cloth left over from my doll's dress," went on Janet. "I'll get that for you."

"Thanks," murmured Ted. "I guess girls do know something about snow men," he added to Tom.

"Course they do," the other boy agreed. "I like your sister Janet."

Ted began to feel that, even if Janet was a year younger than he, she might be smarter in some ways than he was. He was sure of it when he saw how well the snow man looked with his red tongue and lips which Tom made from the scarlet cloth Jan gave him.

"Now if we only had a hat for him he'd look great!" cried Ted, when the last touches were being put on the snow man, even ears having been given him, though, of course, he could not hear through them.

"I know where there's an old hat—a big stovepipe one," said Jan. She meant a tall, shiny, silk hat.

"Where is it?" asked Tom.

"Up in our attic. Daddy used to wear it, mother said, but it's too old-fashioned now. Maybe she'd let us take it."

Mrs. Martin said the children might have the old tall hat, which was broken in one place, but the snow man did not mind that. It was soon perched on his head and then a very proper figure indeed he looked, as he stood up straight and stiff in the yard back of the house.

More than one person stopped to look at what the Curlytops had made and many smiled as they saw the tall silk hat on the snow man. He even had a cane, made from a stick, and he was altogether a very proper and stylish snow man.

Trouble seemed to think the white man with his shiny black hat, was made for him to play with, for no sooner was it finished than Baby

51

William began throwing snowballs at "Mr. North," as Mrs. Martin said they ought to call the gentleman made from white flakes.

"Oh, you mustn't do that!" cried Ted, as he saw what his little brother was doing. "You'll hit his hat," for one of Trouble's snowballs came very near the shiny "stovepipe" as Jan had called it.

"Trouble 'ike snow man," said the little fellow, laughing.

"Well, we like him, too," answered Janet, "and we don't want you to spoil him, baby. Don't throw snowballs at Mr. North."

"Here, I'll help you make a little snow man for yourself," offered Ted to his brother.

"Oh, dat fun!" laughed the little fellow. "I want a biggest one."

"No, a small one will be better, and then you can throw as many snowballs at it as you want," went on Ted.

Jan helped Ted make the snow man for Trouble, for Tom and Lola were called home by their mother. In a short while Trouble's white image was finished. Jan found more red cloth to make the lips and tongue, Ted got more coal for eyes and coat buttons and then he made a paper soldier hat for the small snow man.

"Do you like it, Trouble?" asked his brother, when it was finished.

"Nice," answered Baby William. "Bring it in house to play wif!"

"Oh, no! You mustn't try to do that!" laughed Janet. "If you brought your snow man into the house he would all melt!"

"All melt away?" asked the little fellow.

"Yes, all melt into water. He has to stay out where it's cold. Play with him out here, Trouble."

So Trouble did, making a lot of snowballs which he piled around the feet of his man, so that they might be ready in case the snow man himself wanted to throw them.

Then Teddy and Janet went coasting just before supper, coming home with red cheeks and sparkling eyes, for it was cold and they had played hard.

"Well, Trouble, is the snow man all right?" asked Ted, as he and Jan sat down to supper a little later.

HE WAS ALTOGETHER A VERY STYLISH SNOW MAN.

"Iss. Big snow man in yard," answered Baby William.

"He'll take care of your little snow man all night," added Janet. "Then your little snow man won't be afraid to stay out in the dark, Trouble."

"Trouble's snow man not be in dark," was the answer. "He gone bed. Trouble's snow man gone bed."

"What does he mean?" asked Ted.

"Oh, I presume he's just pretending that he put his snow man to bed in a drift of snow," said Mrs. Martin. "The poor child is so sleepy from having played out all the afternoon that he can't keep his eyes open. I'll put you to bed right after supper, Trouble."

"Trouble go to bed—snow man go to bed," murmured Baby William. He was very sleepy, so much so that his head nodded even while he was eating the last of his bread and milk. And then his mother carried him off to his room.

Ted and Janet sat up a little later to talk to their father, as they generally did.

"Did you hear any more from Grandpa Martin?" asked Ted, after he had finished studying his school lesson for the next day.

"What about?" asked Mr. Martin.

"About the big snowstorm that's coming."

"Oh, you mean about what the hermit said," laughed his father. "No, we haven't had any more letters from grandpa."

"But we will have enough to eat even if we are snowed in, won't we?" Jan queried.

"Oh, yes, I guess so," answered Daddy Martin. "Don't worry about that."

"Can those hermits really tell when there's going to be a big storm with lots of snow?" asked Ted.

"Well, sometimes," admitted Mr. Martin. "Men who live in the woods or mountains all their lives know more about the weather

54

than those of us who live in houses in towns or cities most of the time. Sometimes the hermits and woodsmen can tell by the way the squirrels and other animals act and store away food, whether or not it is going to be a hard winter. But don't worry about being snowed in. If we are we'll make the best of it."

A little later Ted and Jan, still thinking what would happen if a storm should come heavy enough to cover the house, started for their bedrooms. As Janet undressed and turned back the covers of her bed she gave a scream.

"What's the matter?" asked her mother from the hall.

"Maybe she saw a baby mouse!" laughed Ted.

"Oh, no. Mother! Daddy! Come quick!" cried Jan. "There's somebody in my bed!"

Mrs. Martin ran into her little girl's room, and there, on the white sheet, half covered, she saw a strange bedfellow.

CHAPTER VIII
THE LAME BOY

"OH, what is it? What is it?" cried Jan, backing into the farthest corner of her room. "What's in my bed?"

"It's a man!" cried Ted, who had run in from his room. "Oh, Daddy, there's a man in Jan's bed!" he shouted down the stairs.

"It can't be—it isn't large enough for a man!" said Mrs. Martin, who was going toward the gas jet to turn it higher.

Her husband dropped the paper he had been reading as the children were getting ready for bed, and came racing up the stairs. Into Jan's room he went, and, as he entered, Mrs. Martin turned the light on so that it shone more brightly.

Daddy Martin gave one look into Jan's bed and then began to laugh.

"Oh, Daddy! what is it?" cried the little girl. "Is it a man in my bed?"

"Yes," answered her father, still laughing. "But it's a very little man, and he couldn't hurt anybody."

"Not if he was a—a burglar?" asked Ted in a whisper.

"No; for he's only a snow man!" laughed Mr. Martin.

"A *snow* man!" exclaimed Mrs. Martin.

"A snow man in my bed!" gasped Jan. "How did he get there?"

By this time so much noise had been made that Trouble, in his mother's room, was awakened. He came toddling into Jan's room, rubbing his sleepy eyes and holding up his little nightdress so he would not stumble over it.

"Dis mornin'?" he asked, blinking at the bright lights.

"No, it isn't morning, Trouble," answered his mother with a laugh. "But I guess Jan will have to sleep in your bed and you'll have to

56

come in with me. The snow man has melted, making a little puddle of water and her sheets are all wet. She can't sleep in that bed."

They all gathered around to look at the strange sight in Jan's bed. As her mother had said, the snow man, which was about two feet long, had melted. One of his legs was half gone, an ear had slid off and his nose was quite flat, while one of the pieces of coal that had pretended to be an eye had dropped out and was resting on his left shoulder.

"Dat *my* snow man!" announced Trouble, after a look. "Me put him s'eepin's in Jan's bed!"

"You did?" cried Mother Martin. "Well, it's a good thing you told us, for I was going to ask Ted if he had done it as a joke."

"No'm, Mother; I didn't do it!" declared Ted.

"And it is the little snow man we helped Trouble make," added Jan, as she took another look. "I couldn't see good at first 'cause it was so dark in my room. But it's Trouble's snow man."

"Did you really bring him in and put him to sleep in Jan's bed?" asked Baby William's father.

"Iss, I did," answered Trouble, still rubbing his eyes. "My snow man not want to stay out in dark cold all night alone. Big snow man might bite him. I bringed him in wif my two arms, I did, and I did put him in Jan's bed, I did. He go s'eepin's."

"Well, he's slept enough for to-night," said Mr. Martin, still laughing. "Out of the window you go!" he cried, and raising the sash near the head of Jan's bed he tossed the snow man—or what was left of him—out on the porch roof.

"Here, Nora!" called Mrs. Martin. "Please take the wet clothes off Jan's bed so they'll dry. The mattress is wet, too, so she can't sleep on it. Oh, you're a dear bunch of Trouble!" she cried as she caught Baby William up in her arms and kissed his sleepy eyes, "but you certainly made lots of work to-night. What made you put the snow man in Jan's bed?"

"So him have good s'eepin's. Him very twired an' s'eepy out in de yard. I bringed him in, I did!"

"Well, don't do it again," said Mr. Martin, and then they all went to bed, and the snow man—what was left of him—slept out on the roof, where he very likely felt better than in a warm room, for men made of snow do not like the heat.

"Well, Trouble, what are you going to do to-day?" asked his father. He was just finishing his breakfast and Baby William had just started his.

"Trouble goin' make nudder snow man," was the answer.

"Well, if you do, don't put it in my bed," begged Jan, with a laugh.

"Put him in wif Nicknack," went on Trouble.

"Yes, I guess our goat doesn't mind snow, the way he butted into our house," observed Ted.

"Oh, aren't we going to build another ever?" asked Jan. "It was lots of fun. Let's make another house, Ted."

"All right, maybe we will after school. It looks maybe as if it would snow again."

"We have had more snowstorms than we usually do at this time of the year," remarked Mrs. Martin. "I guess Grandpa Martin's old hermit told part of the truth, anyhow."

"Come on, Jan!" cried Ted to his sister, as they left the table to get ready for school. "We'll have a lot of fun in the snow to-day."

"Will we go coasting or skating?" Janet asked.

"There isn't any skating, unless we clean the snow off the pond," replied Ted. "And that's an awful lot of work," he added. "When we come home from school we'll build a great big snow house, if the snow is soft enough to pack."

"On your way home from school," said Mrs. Martin to Ted and Jan, "I want you to stop at your father's store. He'll take you to get new rubber boots. Your old ones are nearly worn out, and if we are to have much snow this winter you'll need bigger ones to keep your feet dry. So stop at daddy's store. He'll be looking for you."

"New rubber boots!" cried Ted. "That's dandy!"

"Oh, may I have a high pair?" asked Jan. "I want to wade in drifts as high as Ted does, and I can't if you get me low boots."

"Your father will get you the right kind," said Mrs. Martin. "The boot store is near his, and he'll go in to buy them with you."

Jan and Ted were very glad they were going to have new rubber boots, and Ted was thinking so much about his that when his teacher in school asked him how to spell foot he spelled "b-o-o-t!"

The other boys and girls laughed, and at first Ted did not know why. But, after a bit, when he saw the teacher smiling also, he remembered what he had done. Then he spelled foot correctly.

"Theodore was thinking more of what to put on his foot, than about the word I asked him to spell," said the teacher.

Mr. Martin's store was not far from the school, and Ted and Jan hurried there when their lessons were over.

"Where you goin'?" asked Tom Taylor, as he came running out of the school yard. "Come on, Curlytop, and let's make another snow man."

"I will after I get my new rubber boots," promised Ted. "You can start making it in our yard if you want to. But don't let Trouble make any more little snow men. He put one in my sister's bed last night."

"He did?" laughed Tom. "Say, he's queer all right!"

"Well, Curlytops, did you come to buy out the store?" asked Mr. Martin with a laugh as he saw his two children come in and walk back toward the end, where he had his office.

"We want rubber boots," said Ted.

"And I want big high ones, just like those he's going to have," begged Jan, pointing to her brother.

"We'll get them just alike and then you won't have any trouble," laughed her father. "Only, of course, Ted's will have to be a little larger in the feet than yours, Jan."

"Oh, yes, Daddy! That's all right," and she smiled. "But I want mine high up on my legs."

Telling one of his clerks to stay in the office until he came back, Mr. Martin took Ted and Jan to the shoestore a few doors down the street. There were many other boys and girls, and men and women, too, getting boots or rubbers.

"Well, Mr. Martin," said the clerk who had come to wait on the Curlytops, "I see you're getting ready for a hard winter. If you get snowed in out at your house, these youngsters can wade out and buy a loaf of bread."

"We're going to have a lot to eat in our house," put in Ted, "'cause a hermit my grandpa knows said we might get snowed in."

"Indeed!" exclaimed the clerk. "Well, it looks as though we would have plenty of snow. We've had more so far this year than we did in twice as long a time last season. Now about your rubber boots," and he took the measure of the feet of Ted and Jan, and soon fitted them with high boots, lined with red flannel.

"Do they suit you, Jan?" asked her father.

"Yes, they're just right," she answered. "I like 'em!"

"They're fine!" cried Ted, stretching out his legs as he sat on the bench in the shoestore. "Now I can wade in deep drifts," for the boots could be strapped around his legs at the top, as could Jan's, and no snow could get down inside.

"Well, run along home and have fun in the snow!" said their father. "Oh, I forgot something! Come on back to the store a minute. I bought a new kind of chocolate candy to-day and I thought maybe you might like to try it."

"Oh, Daddy! We would!" cried Jan, clapping her hands.

"Mind you! I'm not *sure* you'll like it," her father said, trying not to smile, "but if you *don't*, just save it for Nicknack. He isn't particular about candy."

"Oh, we'll like it all right!" laughed Ted. "Hurry, Jan. I'm hungry for candy now!"

The chocolate was very good, and Ted and Jan each had as large a piece as was good for them, and some to take home to their mother, with a little bite for Trouble. As the Curlytops were getting ready to leave their father's store the clerk came from the office and said:

"While you were gone, Mr. Martin, a lame boy came in here to see you."

"A lame boy?" Mr. Martin was much surprised.

"Yes. He said he had been in a Home up near Cherry Farm, where you were last summer," went on the clerk.

"What did he want?" asked Mr. Martin.

"I don't know. He didn't say, but stated that he would wait until you came back. So I gave him a chair just outside the office. He seemed to know about you and Ted and Jan."

"A lame boy! Oh, maybe it was Hal Chester!" cried Jan.

"But Hal isn't lame any more," Mr. Martin reminded her. "At least he is only a little lame. Did this boy limp much?" he asked the clerk.

"Well, not so very much. He seemed anxious to see you, though."

"Where is he?" asked Mr. Martin. "I'll be glad to see him. Where is he now?"

"That's what I don't know. I had to leave the office a minute, and when I came back he was gone."

"Gone?"

"Yes, he wasn't here at all. And, what is more, something went with him."

"What do you mean?" asked Mr. Martin.

"I mean the lame boy took with him a pocketbook and some money when he went out," answered the clerk.

CHAPTER IX
THROUGH THE ICE

MR. MARTIN said nothing for a few seconds after hearing what his clerk told him. Ted and Jan looked at each other. They did not know what to say.

"Are you sure the lame boy took the pocketbook and the money?" asked the Curlytops' father of his clerk.

"Pretty sure; yes, sir. The pocketbook—it was a sort of wallet I had some papers in besides money—was left on this bench right near where he was sitting while he was waiting for you. I went away and when I came back he was gone and so was the pocketbook. He must have taken it."

"Was there much money in it?"

"Only about fifteen dollars."

"That's too bad. I wonder what the boy wanted. Didn't he say?"

"Not to me, though to one of the other clerks who spoke to him as he sat near the bench he said he was in need of help."

"Then it couldn't have been Hal Chester," said Mr. Martin, "for his father is able to provide for him. Besides, Hal wouldn't go away without waiting to see Ted and Jan, for they had such good times together at Cherry Farm and on Star Island.

"Hal Chester," went on Mr. Martin to the clerk, who had never been to Cherry Farm, "was a lame boy who was almost cured at the Home for Crippled Children not far from my father's house. He left there to go to his own home about the time we broke up our camp. I don't see why he would come here to see me."

"Maybe his father lost all his money and Hal wanted to see if you'd give him more," suggested Jan.

"Or maybe he wanted to get work in your store," added Ted.

"I hardly think so," remarked his father. "It is queer, though, why the boy should go away without seeing me, whoever he was. I'm sorry about the missing pocketbook. I know Hal would never do such a thing as that. Well, it can't be helped."

"Shall I call the police?" asked the clerk.

"What for?" Mr. Martin queried.

"So they can look for this lame boy, whoever he was, and arrest him for taking that money."

"Maybe he didn't take it," said Mr. Martin.

"He must have," declared the clerk. "The pocketbook was right on the bench near him, and after he went away the pocketbook wasn't there any more. He took it all right!"

"Well, never mind about the police for a while," said the children's father. "Maybe the lame boy will come back and tell us what he wanted to see me about, and maybe he only took the pocketbook by mistake. Or some one else may have walked off with it. Don't call the police yet."

"I'm glad daddy didn't call the police," said Ted to Jan, as they went home a little later, carrying their fine, new, rubber boots.

"So'm I," agreed his sister. "Even if it was Hal I don't believe he took the money."

"No, course not! Hal wouldn't do that. Anyhow Hal wasn't hardly lame at all any more. The doctors at the Home cured him," said Ted.

"Unless maybe he got lame again in the snow," suggested Janet.

"Well, of course he might have slipped down and hurt his foot," admitted Ted. "But anyhow I guess it wasn't Hal."

Neither of the Curlytops liked to think that their former playmate would do such a thing as to take a pocketbook that did not belong to him. Mother Martin, when told what had happened at the store that day, said she was sure it could not be Hal.

"There's one way you can find out," she said to her husband. "Write to Hal's father and ask him if he has been away from home."

"I'll do it!" agreed Mr. Martin, while Ted and Jan were out in the snow, wading in the biggest drifts they could find with their high rubber boots on. Their feet did not get a bit wet.

In a few days Mr. Martin had an answer from the letter he had sent to Mr. Chester, Hal's father. The letter was written by a friend of Mr. Chester's who was in charge of his home and who opened all the mail. Mr. Chester, this man wrote, was traveling with his wife and Hal, and no one knew just where they were at present.

"Then it might have been Hal, after all, who called at your office," said Mrs. Martin to her husband. "He may have been near here, and wanted to stop to see the children, and, not knowing where we lived, he inquired for your store. But if it was Hal I'm perfectly sure he didn't take the pocketbook."

"So am I," said Mr. Martin. "And yet we haven't found it at the store, nor was there anyone else near it while the lame boy was sitting on the bench. It's too bad! I'd like to find out who he was and what he wanted of me."

But, for the present, there seemed no way to do this. Ted and Jan wondered, too, for they would have liked to see Hal again, and they did not, even for a moment, believe he had taken the money. Hal Chester was not that kind of boy.

The Curlytops had much fun in the snow. They went riding down hill whenever they could, and made more snow men and big snowballs. Ted and Tom Taylor talked of building a big snow house, much larger than the first one they had made.

"And we'll pour water over the walls, and make them freeze into ice," said Ted. "Then Nicknack can't butt 'em down with his horns."

But there was not quite enough snow around the Martin yard to make the large house the boys wanted, so they decided to wait until more of the white flakes fell.

"There'll be plenty of snow," said Ted to his chum. "My father had another letter from my grandfather, and he says the hermit said a terribly big storm was coming in about two weeks."

"Whew!" whistled Tom Taylor. "I guess I'd better go home and tell my mother to get in plenty of bread and butter and jam. I like that; don't you?"

"I guess I do!" cried Ted. "I'm going in now and ask Nora if she'll give us some. I'm awful hungry!"

Nora took pity on Ted and the other boy who was playing in the yard with him, and they were soon sitting on the back steps eating bread and jam.

They had each taken about three bites from the nice, big slices Nora had given them, when around the back walk came a man who was limping on one leg, the other being of wood. Though the man's clothes were ragged, and he seemed to be what would be called a "tramp," he had a kind face, though as Ted said afterward, it had on it more whiskers than ever his father's had. Still the man seemed to be different from the ordinary tramps.

"Ah, that's what I like to see!" he exclaimed as he watched the boys eating the bread and jam. "Nothing like that for the appetite—I mean to take away an appetite—when you've got more than you need."

"Have you got an appetite?" asked Tom Taylor.

"Indeed I have," answered the man. "I've got more appetite than I know what to do with. I was just going to ask if you thought I could get something to eat here. Having an appetite means you're hungry, you know," he added with a smile, so Ted and Tom would understand. The man looked hungrily at the bread and jam the boys were eating.

"Would you—would you like some of *this*?" asked Teddy, holding out his slice, which had three bites and a half taken from it. The half bite was the one Ted took just as he saw the man. He was so surprised that he took only a half bite instead of a whole one.

"Would I like that? Only just wouldn't I, though!" cried the man, smacking his lips. "But please don't ask me," he went on. "It isn't good for the appetite to see things and not eat 'em."

"You can eat this," said Teddy, as he held out his slice of bread and jam. "I've taken only a few bites out of it. And I cleaned my teeth this morning," he added as if that would make it all right that he had eaten part of the slice.

"Oh, that part doesn't worry me!" laughed the tramp. "But I don't want, hungry as I am, to take your bread and butter, to say nothing of the jam."

He turned aside and then swung back.

"There is butter on the bread, under that jam, isn't there?" he asked.

"Yes," answered Tom. "It's good butter, too."

"So I should guess," went on the man. "I can most always tell when there's butter on the bread under the jam. There's always one sure way to tell," he said.

"How?" asked Ted, thinking it might be some trick.

"Just take a *bite*!" laughed the man, and the two boys on the back steps laughed, too.

"Are you sure you don't want this?" the tramp went on, as he took the partly eaten slice Ted held out to him. "I wouldn't for the world, hungry as I am, take your slice——"

"Oh, Nora'll give me more," said Ted eagerly. He really wanted to see the man bite into the slice. Ted said afterward that he wanted to know how big a bite the man could take.

"Well, then, if you can get more I will take this," said the man, as he eagerly and, so it seemed to the boys, very hungrily bit into the slice—or what was left of it after Ted had taken out his three and a half nibbles. What Ted took were really nibbles alongside the bites the man took.

"Were you in a war?" asked Tom, as he watched the tramp take the last of Ted's bread.

"No. Why did you think I was—because I have a wooden leg?"

The boy nodded.

"My leg was cut off on the railroad," went on the tramp. "But I get along pretty well on this wooden peg. It's a good thing in a way, too," he added.

"How's that?" asked Tom.

"Well, you see havin' only one leg there isn't so much of me to get hungry. It's just like having only one mouth instead of two. If you boys had two mouths you'd have to have two slices of bread and jam instead of one," went on the tramp, laughing. "It's the same way when you only have one leg instead of two—you don't get so hungry."

"Are you hungry yet?" asked Tom, as he saw the tramp licking off with his tongue some drops of jam that got on his fingers.

"I am," the man answered. "My one leg isn't quite full yet—I mean my one good leg," he added. "You can't put anything—not even bread and jam into this wooden peg," and he tapped it with his cane.

"Take my slice of bread," said Tom kindly. "I guess I can get some more when I get home."

"Nora'll give you some same as she will me," said Teddy. "Go on and eat—I like to watch you," he added to the tramp.

"Well, you don't like to watch me any more than I like to do it," laughed the ragged man, as he began on the second slice of bread and jam.

He ate that all up, and then, when Teddy and Tom went in and told Nora what had happened, the good-natured girl insisted on getting some hot coffee and bread and meat for the hungry man.

JAN WENT THROUGH THE ICE INTO THE BLACK WATER.

"Jam and such like isn't anything near enough," she said, "even if he has but one leg. I'll feed him proper."

Which she did, and the tramp with the "wooden peg," as he called it, was very thankful. Before he left he cut some wood for Nora, and also whittled out two little wooden swords for Ted and Tom.

"I'm glad we gave him our bread and jam; aren't you?" asked Ted of his chum.

"Yep," was the answer. "I liked him, and it was fun to see him take big bites."

A snowstorm came a few days later, and, for a time, the Curlytops thought it might be the big one Grandpa Martin's hermit had spoken of. But the snow soon changed to rain and then came a thaw, so that there was not a bit of snow left on the ground, all being washed away.

"Oh, dear!" sighed Jan, as she looked out of the window. "This isn't like winter at all! We can't have any fun!"

"Wait till it freezes," said Ted. "Then we'll have lots of fun skating on the pond."

Two nights later there came a cold spell, and the ice formed on the pond. But, though the Curlytops did not know it, the ice was not as thick as it ought to have been to make it safe.

On the big lake, where the larger boys and girls went skating, a man, sent by the chief of police, always tested the ice after a freeze, to make sure it was thick enough to hold up the crowds of skaters. But on the pond, where the water was not more than knee-deep, no one ever looked at the ice. The little boys and girls went there just as they pleased.

"Come on skating!" cried Ted, after school the first day of this cold weather. "We'll have a race on the ice, Jan."

"All right," she answered. "I can skate faster than you if I am a girl!"

"No, you can't!" exclaimed Ted.

"I want to come!" cried Trouble, as he saw his brother and sister starting out with their skates on straps over their shoulders.

"Oh, no! You're too little!" said his mother. "You must stay with me."

But Trouble did not wish to do that, and cried until Nora came in and said he might help her bake a cake. This pleased the little fellow, who, if he were given a piece of dough, not too sticky, to play with, had a fine time imagining he was making pies or a cake.

So Ted and Janet hurried off to the pond and were soon skating away with other boys and girls of their own age and size.

"Come on, now, let's race!" cried Ted, after a bit. "I'll get to the other side of the pond 'fore you do, Jan!"

"No, you won't!" she exclaimed, and the Curlytops started off on their race, the others watching.

For a while Ted was ahead, and then, whether it was because she was a better skater or because her skates were sharper, Jan passed her brother. He tried to catch up to her but could not.

And then, when Jan was about twenty feet ahead of Teddy and in the middle of the pond, the ice suddenly began to crack.

"Look out! Come on back! You'll go through!" cried Tom Taylor.

"Oh, she's in now!" screamed Lola.

And, as Lola spoke, Jan went through the ice into the black water beneath.

"Skate to shore! Skate to shore!" called Tom to the others. "Get off the ice or you'll go in, too!"

The other children did as he said, and it was well that they did, for the ice was now cracking in all directions from the big hole in the middle, through which Janet had gone down.

Teddy, who was skating as hard as he could, could not stop himself at once, but went on, straight for the hole through which his sister had slipped.

"Stop! Stop!" yelled Tom, waving his hands at Ted. "Stop!"

Ted tried to, digging the back point of his skate into the ice as he had seen other skaters do when they wanted to stop quickly. But he was going too fast to come to a halt soon enough, and it looked as though he, also, would go into the water.

"Fall down and slide! Fall down!" cried a bigger boy who had come over to see if his own little brother was all right on the pond.

Ted understood what this boy meant. By falling down on the ice and sliding, he would not go as fast, and he might stop before he got to the hole where the black water looked so cold and wet.

Flinging his feet from under him Ted dropped full length on the frozen pond, but still he felt himself sliding toward the hole. He could see Janet now. She was trying to stand up and she was crying and sobbing.

CHAPTER X
THANKSGIVING

"LOOK out, Teddy! Look out, or you'll fall in same as I did!"

This is what Janet Martin called to her brother as she saw him sliding toward her when she was in the pond where she had broken through the ice. She stopped crying and shivering from the icy water long enough to say that.

"Stop, Teddy! Stop!" she shouted.

"I'm tryin' to!" he answered. He pressed hard with his mittened hands on the smooth ice on which he had thrown himself. It was very slippery. He was sliding ahead feet first and he could lift up his head and look at his sister.

Luckily the water was not deep in the pond—hardly over Janet's knees—and when she had fallen through the ice she had managed to stand up. Her feet, with the skates still on them, were down in the soft mud and ooze of the pond, the bottom of which had not frozen.

"I can't stop!" yelled Teddy, and it did seem as though he would go into the water also. But he stopped just in time, far enough away from the hole to prevent his going through the ice, which had cracked in three or more places.

"Crawl back to shore!" yelled the big boy, named Ford Henderson, who had come to look after his own little brother, whom he found safe. "Crawl back to shore, Curlytop. Don't stand up, or you might fall down where the ice is thin and crack a hole in it. Crawl back to shore!"

"But I want to help Janet!" said Teddy, who was almost ready to cry himself, since he saw in what plight his sister Janet now was.

"I'll get her out!" called Ford.

Then, while Teddy slowly crawled back over the ice, which every now and then cracked a little, as if the whole frozen top of the pond were going to fall in, Ford, the big boy, not in the least minding his feet getting wet, ran to where Janet stood up in the hole. Ford broke through the ice also, but as he was quite tall the water did not even come to his knees.

"Don't cry. You'll be all right soon," said Ford in a kind voice to the little girl. "I'll take you home!"

Then, being strong, he lifted her up in his arms, skates and all, and, with the mud and water dripping from her feet while his own were soaking wet, the big boy ran toward the Martin home with Janet.

"You come along, too, Curlytop!" called Ford to Teddy. "If I bring in your sister, all wet from having fallen through the ice, your mother will be afraid you are drowned. Come along!"

So Teddy, quickly taking off his skates, Tom Taylor helping him, ran along beside Ford, who was carrying Janet. The other boys and girls who had run from the cracking ice in time to get off before they broke through, followed, so there was quite a procession coming toward the Martin house. Mrs. Martin, looking out of the window, saw it and, seeing Jan being carried by the big boy, guessed at once what had happened.

"Oh, my goodness!" she cried to Nora. "Jan has fallen through the ice. She'll be soaking wet and cold. Get some hot water ready, and I'll bring some blankets to warm. She must be given a hot bath and put to bed in warm clothes. Maybe Teddy is wet, too, or some of the others. Hurry, Nora!"

And Nora hurried as she never had before, so that by the time Ford had set Jan down in a chair by the stove in the kitchen and had helped Mrs. Martin take off her wet skates and shoes, the water was ready and Janet was given a hot foot bath.

"You must dry yourself, Ford," said Mrs. Martin. "I can't thank you enough for saving my little girl!"

"Oh, she was all right," answered Ford. "She stood up herself, because the water wasn't deep, and I just lifted her out of the mud. Ted did well, too, for he stopped himself from going into the hole."

"I was going to get Janet out," Teddy answered.

"I knew you would be a brave little boy when your sister was in danger," said Mrs. Martin. "Now here is some hot milk for you, Janet, and I guess you're old enough to have a little coffee, Ford. It will keep you from catching cold I hope."

"Couldn't he have some bread and jam with it, Mother?" asked Janet, as she sipped her warm drink. "Maybe he's hungry."

"Maybe he is!" laughed Mrs. Martin.

"Oh, don't bother!" exclaimed Ford.

But Mrs. Martin got it ready and Ford ate the bread and jam as though he liked it. So did Ted, and then Nora took some cookies out to the boys and girls from the pond who had gathered in front of the Martin home to talk about Janet's having gone through the ice and of how Ford had pulled her out of the mud.

Altogether there was a great deal of excitement, and many people in town talked about the Curlytops that night when the boys and girls went to their homes with the news.

"Some one ought to look after the ice on the little pond as well as on the lake when there is skating," said Mr. Martin, when he heard what had happened. "We want our little boys and girls to be safe as well as the larger ones. I'll see about it."

So he did, and after that, for the rest of the winter and each winter following, a man was sent to see how thick the ice on the little pond was, and if it would not hold up a big crowd of little boys and girls none was allowed on until it had frozen more thickly.

"But when are we going to build the big snow house?" asked Jan one night at supper, when she and Ted had played hard on the hill after school.

"You can't build it until there's more snow," said her mother. "You'll have to wait until another storm comes. I expect there'll be one soon, for Thanksgiving is next week, and we usually have a good snow then."

75

"Oh, is it Thanksgiving?" cried Ted. "What fun we'll have!"

"Is grandpa or grandma coming to see us this year?" asked Jan.

"No, they have to stay on Cherry Farm. I asked them to come, but grandpa says if there is going to be a blizzard, and any danger of his getting snowed in, he wants to be at home where he can feed the cows and horses."

"Aren't we going to have any company over Thanksgiving?" asked Ted.

"Well, maybe," and his mother smiled.

"Oh, somebody is coming!" cried Jan joyfully. "It's going to be a surprise, Ted! I can tell by the way mother laughs with her eyes!"

"Is it going to be a surprise?" Ted asked.

"Well, maybe," and Mrs. Martin laughed.

The weather grew colder as Thanksgiving came nearer. There were two or three flurries of snow, but no big storm, though Jan and Ted looked anxiously for one, as they wanted a big pile of the white flakes in the yard so they could make a snow house.

"We'll make the biggest one ever!" declared Ted. "And maybe we'll turn it into a fort and have an Indian fight!"

"I don't like Indian fights," said Janet.

"They'll only be make-believe," Ted went on. "Me an' Tom Taylor an' some of the fellows'll be the Indians."

But the big snow held off, though each morning, as soon as they arose from their beds, Jan and Ted would run to the window to look out to see if it had come in the night. There was just a little covering of white on the ground, and in some places, along the streets and the sidewalks, it had been shoveled away.

"Do you think it will snow for Thanksgiving?" asked the Curlytops again and again.

"Yes, I think so," their mother would answer.

Such busy times as there were at the Martin house! Mrs. Martin and Nora were in the kitchen most of each day, baking, boiling, frying, stewing and cooking in other ways. There was to be a pumpkin pie, of course—in fact two or three of them, as well as pies of mincemeat and of apple.

"There must be a lot of company coming," said Ted to Janet; "'cause they're bakin' an awful lot."

"Well, everybody eats a lot at Thanksgiving," said the little girl. "Only I hope we have snow and lots of company."

"Did you hear anything more about the lame boy and the missing pocketbook and money?" asked Mrs. Martin of her husband two or three days before Thanksgiving.

"No, not a thing," he answered. "He did not come back to the store, and we haven't found the lost money. I am hoping we shall, though, for, though I can't guess who the lame boy was, if he wasn't Hal, I wouldn't want to think any little chap would take what did not belong to him."

"Nor would I," said the Curlytops' mother.

The next afternoon something queer happened. Teddy and Janet had not yet come home from school, and Mrs. Martin and Nora were in the kitchen baking the last of the things for Thanksgiving and getting things ready to roast the big turkey which would come the next day.

The front doorbell rang and Mrs. Martin said:

"You'd better answer, Nora. My hands are covered with flour."

"And so is my nose," answered the maid with a laugh. "You look better to go to the front door than I do."

"Well, I guess I do," agreed Mrs. Martin with a smile. She paused to wipe her hands on a towel and then went through the hall. But when she opened the door no one was on the steps.

"That's queer," she said to herself, looking up and down the street. "I wonder if that could have been Teddy or Jan playing a joke." Then she looked at the clock and noticed that it was not yet time for the children to come home from school.

A man passing in the street saw Mrs. Martin gazing up and down the sidewalk.

"Are you looking for someone?" he asked.

"Well, someone just rang my bell," answered Mrs. Martin. "But I don't see anyone."

"I saw a lame boy go up on your veranda a few minutes ago," went on the man. "He stood there, maybe four or five seconds and then rang the bell. All at once he seemed frightened, and down he hurried off the steps and ran around the corner, limping."

"He did?" cried Mrs. Martin. "Why, how strange! Did he say anything to you?"

"No, I wasn't near enough, but I thought it queer."

"It is queer," agreed Mrs. Martin. "I wonder who he was, and if he is in sight now?"

She ran down the steps and hurried around the corner to look down the next street. But no boy, lame or not, was in sight.

"Maybe he was just playing a trick," said the man. "Though he didn't look like that kind of boy."

"No, I think it was no trick," answered the mother of the Curlytops, as she went back into the house.

"What was it?" asked Nora.

"A lame boy, but he ran away after ringing," answered Mrs. Martin. "I wonder if it could have been the boy who was at Mr. Martin's store, and who might know something about the stolen pocketbook, even if he did not take it. Perhaps he came to tell us something about it and, at the last minute, he was too frightened and ran away."

She told this to Mr. Martin when he came home, and he said it might be so.

"If it is," he went on, "that lame boy must be in town somewhere. I'd like to find him. I'll speak to the police. The poor boy may be in trouble."

The police promised to look for the lame boy and help him if he needed it. And then all else was forgotten, for a time, in the joys of the coming Thanksgiving.

The night before the great day, when the Curlytops were in the sitting-room after supper talking of the fun they would have, and when Trouble was going to sleep in his mother's lap, Daddy Martin went to the window to look out.

"It's snowing hard," he said.

"Oh, goodie!" laughed Jan.

"Now we can build the big snow house!" cried Ted.

Just then the doorbell rang loudly.

CHAPTER XI
THE SNOW BUNGALOW

"WHO'S that?" asked Mrs. Martin, without thinking, for, of course, there was no way of telling who was at the door until it was opened.

"I'll go to see," offered Daddy Martin.

"Oh, maybe it's that queer lame boy," suggested Ted.

"Don't let him get away until you talk to him," cautioned Mother Martin. "I'd like to know who he is."

"Whoever is there doesn't seem to be going to run away," remarked the Curlytops' father. "They're stamping the snow off their feet as if they intended to come in."

"Oh, I wonder if it could be *them*?" said Mrs. Martin questioningly.

"Who, Mother? Who do you think it is?" asked Jan, but her mother did not answer. She stood in the hall while her husband went to the door. Outside could be heard the voices of people talking.

Then the door was opened by Mr. Martin, letting in a cloud of snowflakes and a blast of cold air that made the Curlytops shiver in the warm house.

"Well, here we are!" cried a jolly voice.

"Sort of a surprise!" some one else added; a woman's voice Jan decided. The other was a man's.

"Well, how in the world did you get here at this time of night?" asked Daddy Martin in surprise. "Come right in out of the storm. We're glad to see you! Come in and get warm. It's quite a storm, isn't it?"

"Yes. And it's going to be worse," the man's voice said. "It's going to be a regular blizzard, I imagine."

"Oh, goodie!" murmured Ted.

"But who is it—who's come to see us so late at night?" asked Janet.

"Pooh! 'Tisn't late," said her brother. "Only a little after eight o'clock. Oh, it's Aunt Jo!" he cried a moment later as he caught sight of the lady's face when she took off her veil and shook from it the snowflakes.

"Yes, it's Aunt Jo, Curlytop!" cried the lady. "I'd hug you, only I'm wet. But I'll get dry in a minute and then I will. Where's my little Curlytop girl, and where's that dear bunch of Trouble?"

"Here I is!" cried Baby William, who had been awakened when the bell rang. He had been put on the couch by his mother, but now came toddling out into the hall. "Who is it?" he asked, rubbing his sleepy eyes.

"It's Aunt Jo!" cried Ted. "Aunt Jo's come to visit us for Thanksgiving. Oh, I'm so glad!" and Teddy danced wildly about the room.

"And it's Uncle Frank, too!" cried Mother Martin. "You children don't know him as well as you do Aunt Jo, for you haven't seen him so often. But here he is!"

"Is it Uncle Frank from out West where the cowboys and Indians live?" asked Ted, stopping his dance to think of this new interest.

"That's who I am, young man!" answered the hearty voice of the man who had come through the storm with Aunt Jo. "As soon as I shake off this fur coat, which has as much snow on it as a grizzly bear gets on him when he plays tag in a blizzard, I'll have a look at you. There! It's off. Now where are the children with such curly hair? I want to see 'em!"

"Here they are," answered Daddy Martin. "They were just going to bed to get up good appetites for the Thanksgiving dinner to-morrow. But I guess we can let them stay up a little longer. We didn't expect you two until to-morrow."

"We both managed to get earlier trains than we expected," explained Aunt Jo.

"And we met each other at the Junction, without expecting to, and came on together," added Uncle Frank. "Thought we'd give you a surprise."

"Glad you did," returned Mr. Martin. "I was beginning to get afraid, if the storm kept up, that you wouldn't get here for Thanksgiving."

"Wouldn't have missed it for two dozen cow ponies and a wire fence thrown in!" laughed Uncle Frank, in his deep voice. "Now where's that curly hair?"

Jan and Ted, just a little bashful in the presence of their Western uncle, who did not often leave his ranch to come East, went forward. Uncle Frank looked at them, ran his fingers through Ted's tightly curled hair and then cried:

"Oh, I'm caught!"

"What's the matter?" asked Aunt Jo with a laugh.

"My fingers are tangled in Ted's hair and I can't get them loose!" said Uncle Frank, pretending that his hand was held fast. "Say, I heard your hair was curly," he went on, after he had finally gotten his fingers loose, having made believe it was very hard work, "but I never thought it was like this. And Jan's, too! Why, if anything, hers is tighter than Ted's."

"Yes; we call them our Curlytops," said Mother Martin.

"And here's another. His hair isn't curly, though," went on Uncle Frank. "What did you call him?"

"His name is William Anthony Martin," said Aunt Jo. "I know, for I picked out the name."

"But we call him Trouble," said Ted, who was looking eagerly at his big uncle from the West, hoping, perhaps, that he might bring out a gun or a bow and some arrows from the pockets of his fur overcoat. But Uncle Frank did nothing like that.

"Come out in the dining-room and have something to eat," invited Mr. Martin.

"No, thank you. Miss Miller and I had supper before we came here," answered Uncle Frank. "We knew we'd be a little late. But we'll sit and talk a while."

"Mother, may Ted and I stay up and listen—a little bit?" begged Janet.

"Oh, yes, let them, do!" urged Aunt Jo. "It isn't so very late, and they don't have to go to school to-morrow. Besides if this storm keeps up all they can do is to stay in the house."

"We got big rubber boots, and we can go in deep drifts," explained Jan.

"Did you? Well, I guess the drifts will be deeper to-morrow than you've ever seen them if I'm any judge of weather," remarked Uncle Frank. "It's starting in like one of our worst blizzards."

"Then we'll be snowed in like the hermit said we'd be!" cried Ted. "That'll be fun!"

"What does he mean about a hermit?" asked Aunt Jo.

Then Daddy Martin told about the letter from grandpa at Cherry Farm, and of the hermit's prediction that there was going to be a hard winter.

"Well, Thanksgiving is a good time to be snowed in," said Uncle Frank. "There's sure to be enough to eat in the house."

"Were you ever snowed in?" asked Ted, when he was seated on one of Uncle Frank's knees and Jan was on the other.

"Oh, lots of times," was the answer.

"Tell us about it!" eagerly begged the Curlytops.

"I think you had better hear Uncle Frank's stories to-morrow," said Mother Martin. "It is getting late now, and time you were asleep. You may get up early, if you wish and you'll have all day with our nice company."

"Oh, Mother! just let Uncle Frank tell one story!" pleaded Jan.

"We haven't heard one for an awful long while," added her brother. "I mean a story like what he can tell," he added quickly. "Course *you* tell us nice stories, Mother, and so does *Daddy*, but can't Uncle Frank tell us just *one*?"

"I don't know," returned Mother Martin, as if not quite sure.

"Oh, please!" begged Jan and Ted together, for they thought they saw signs of their mother's giving in.

Trouble seemed to know what was going on. He wiggled down from his father's knees and climbed up on those of Uncle Frank. Then he cuddled down in the big man's arms, and the big man seemed to know just how to hold little boys, even if their pet names were like that of Trouble.

"I 'ikes a 'tory!" said Trouble simply. "I 'ikes one very much!"

"Well, now that's too bad," said Uncle Frank with a laugh. "But if daddy and mother say it can't be done, why—it can't!"

"Do you know any short ones?" asked Mr. Martin. "I mean a story that wouldn't keep them up too late, and then keep them awake after they get to bed?"

"Oh, I guess I can dig up a story like that," said Uncle Frank, and he scratched his head, and then stuck one hand down deep in his pocket, as if he intended digging up a story from there.

"Well, I suppose they won't be happy until they hear one," said Mrs. Martin. "So you may tell them one—but let it be short, please."

"All right," agreed Uncle Frank.

"Oh, this is lovely!" murmured Janet.

"What's the story going to be about?" asked Ted.

"What would you like it to be about?" inquired Uncle Frank.

"Tell us of the time you were snowed in," suggested Jan. "And maybe we'll have something like that happen to us."

"Ha! ha!" laughed Uncle Frank. "Well, maybe after you hear about what happened to me you won't want anything like it yourselves. However, here we go!"

He settled himself in the easy chair, cuddled Trouble a little closer to him, and, after looking up at the ceiling, as if to see any part of the story that might be printed there, Uncle Frank began:

"Once upon a time, not so very many years ago— —"

"Oh, I just *love* a story to begin that way; don't you, Ted?" asked Janet.

"Yep. It's great! Go on, Uncle Frank."

"You children mustn't interrupt or Uncle Frank can't tell, or it will take him so much longer that I'll have to put you to bed before the story is finished," said Mother Martin, playfully shaking a finger at Ted and Jan.

"All right, we'll be quiet," promised the little girl.

"Go on, Uncle Frank," begged Teddy.

"Once upon a time, a few years ago," began Uncle Frank the second time, "I was living away out West, farther than I am now, and in a place where hardly anyone else lived. I had just started to make my living in that new country, and I wanted to look about a bit and see a good place to settle in before I built my log cabin.

"I took my gun and rod, as well as something to eat, so I could hunt and fish when I wished, and I set out one day. I traveled over the plains and up and down among the mountains, and one night I found that I was lost."

"Really lost?" asked Jan, forgetting that no questions were allowed.

"Well, I guess you could call it that," said Uncle Frank. "I didn't know where I was, nor the way back to where I had come from, which was a little settlement of miners. There I was, all alone in the mountains, with night coming on, and it was beginning to snow.

"It was cold, too," said Uncle Frank, "and I was glad I had on a fur coat. It wasn't as big as the one I wore here," he said, "but I was very glad to have it, and I buttoned it around me as tight as I could and walked on in the darkness and through the snowstorm, trying to find my way back.

"But I couldn't. I seemed to be getting more lost all the while, and finally I made up my mind there was no help for it. I'd have to stay out in the woods, on top of the mountain all night."

"All alone?" asked Jan.

"All alone," answered Uncle Frank. "But I wasn't afraid, for I had my gun with me, and I'd been out all night alone before that. But I didn't like the cold. I was afraid I might freeze or get snowed in, and then I never could find my way back.

"So, before it got too dark, and before the snow came down too heavily, I stopped, made a little fire and warmed some coffee I had in a tin bottle. I drank that, ate a little cold bread and meat I had, and then I felt better.

"But I wanted some place where I could stay all night. There were no houses where I could go in and get a nice, warm bed. There were no hotels and there wasn't even a log cabin or a shack. I couldn't build a snow house, for the snow was cold and dry and wouldn't pack, so the next best thing to do, I thought, would be for me to find a hollow log and crawl into that.

"So I looked around as well as I could in the storm and darkness," went on Uncle Frank, "and finally I found a log that would just about suit me. I cleared away the snow from one end, kicking it with my boots, and then, when I had buttoned my fur coat around me, I crawled into the log with my gun.

"It was dark inside the hollow log, and not very nice, but it was warm, and I was out of the cold wind and the snow. Of course it was very dark, but as I didn't have anything to read, I didn't need a light.

"After a while I began to feel sleepy, and before I knew it I was dozing off. Just before I began to dream about being in a nice warm house, with some roast turkey and cranberry sauce for supper, I felt some one else getting inside the hollow log with me.

"I was too sleepy to ask who it was. I thought it was somebody like myself, lost in the storm, who had crawled in as I had done to keep from freezing. So I just said: 'Come on, there's lots of room for two of us,' and then I went fast asleep. I thought I'd let the other man sleep, too.

"Well, I stayed in the log all night and then I woke up. I thought it must be morning, but I couldn't see in the dark log. Anyhow, I wanted to get up. So I poked at what I thought was the other man sleeping with me. I poked him again, and I noticed that he had on a fur coat like mine.

"'Come on!' I cried. 'Time to get up!'

"And then, all of a sudden there was a growl and a sniff and a snuff, and, instead of a *man* crawling out the other end of the log, there was a big, shaggy *bear*!"

"Really?" asked Jan, her eyes big with surprise.

"Really and truly," said Uncle Frank.

"Oh! Oh!" gasped Teddy. "Weren't you scared?"

"Well, I didn't have time to be," answered Uncle Frank. "You see, I didn't know it was a bear that had crawled into the log to sleep with me until he crawled out, and there wasn't any use in getting frightened then.

"Out of the log scrambled the bear, and I guess he was as much surprised as I was to find he'd been sleeping in the same hollow-tree-hotel with a man. Away he ran! I could see him running down the hill when I crawled out of the log. Morning had come, the snow had stopped, and I could see to find my way back to the town I had left. But I was glad the bear got in the log with me, for he helped keep me warm. And, all the while, I thought it was another man with a fur coat on like mine.

"There, now that's all the story, and you Curlytops must go to bed! Hello! Trouble's asleep already!"

And so the little fellow was, in Uncle Frank's arms.

"Oh, that was an awful nice story!" said Jan. "Thank you!"

"Yes, it was," added her brother. "I'm awful glad you came to see us," he went on. "I hope you'll stay forever and tell us a story every night. We like stories!"

"Well, one every night would be quite a lot," said his uncle. "But I'll see about it. Anyhow, Aunt Jo and I are glad to be here—at least I am," and Aunt Jo nodded to show that she was also.

"Come, children!" called Mrs. Martin. "Uncle Frank was very good to tell you such a nice, funny story. But now you really must go to bed. To-morrow is another day, and our company will be here then, and for some time longer."

"Did you know they were coming, Mother?" asked Jan, as she slid off her uncle's knee.

"Well, I had an idea," was the smiling answer.

"Is this the surprise daddy was talking about?" Ted queried.

"Yes, this is it," answered his father. "Do you like it?"

"Um, yes!" laughed Ted, and Jan smiled to show that she was of the same mind.

When the Curlytops were in bed Aunt Jo and Uncle Frank told Mr. and Mrs. Martin of their journey. For some time each one had been planning to come to visit their relatives, Aunt Jo from her home in Clayton and Uncle Frank from his Western ranch in Montana. Of course he had started some time before Aunt Jo did, as he had farther to travel. But they both reached the railroad junction, not far from Cresco, at the same time. Then they came the rest of the way together, arriving in the midst of the storm.

"Well, we're glad you're here," said Mrs. Martin, "and the children are delighted. They knew we had some surprise for them, though we did not tell them you were expected. Now I expect they'll hardly sleep, planning things to do in the snow and on the ice."

Indeed Ted and Jan did not go to sleep at once, but talked to each other from their rooms until Mrs. Martin sent Nora up to tell them if they did not get quiet they could not have fun with Aunt Jo and Uncle Frank.

"Oh, it's snowing yet, Jan!" cried Ted, as he jumped out of bed the next morning. "It's going to be a fine storm!"

"That's good!" laughed Janet. "I wonder if Uncle Frank knows how to build a snow house."

"We'll ask him. Come on! Let's hurry down and see if he's up yet."

Uncle Frank was up, and so was Aunt Jo and the whole family, except Trouble, for it was later than the Curlytops thought.

"Make a snow house? Of course I know how!" laughed Uncle Frank. "Many a one I've made out on the prairie when I've been caught in a blizzard."

"Why don't you build a snow bungalow?" asked Aunt Jo.

"What's a bungalow?" asked Jan.

"Well, it's a sort of low, one-story house, with all the rooms on one floor," explained her aunt. "There is no upstairs to it."

"We did build a snow house, and it hadn't any upstairs," said Ted. "But Nicknack, our goat, saw his picture in one of the glass-ice windows, and he butted a hole in the wall."

"Well, he's a great goat!" laughed Uncle Frank. "But if you're going to build another snow house, do as Aunt Jo says, and make it a low bungalow. Then it won't be so easy to knock down. We build low houses out West so the wind storms won't knock them down so easily, and you can pretend your goat is a wind storm."

"That'll be fun!" laughed Ted.

"And we'll make the bungalow with sides and a roof of wood," went on Aunt Jo, "and cover the boards with snow. Then it will look just like a snow house, but it will be stronger. I'll help you. I'm going to build a bungalow myself this summer," she went on, "and I'd like to practise on a snow one first."

"Come on!" cried Ted. "We'll build the snow bungalow!"

"Better get your breakfasts first," said his mother.

This did not take long, for Ted and Jan were anxious to be at their fun. And a little later, with Aunt Jo and Uncle Frank to help, the snow bungalow was started.

CHAPTER XII
TROUBLE IS LOST

"WHAT sort of house are you going to build, Uncle Frank?" asked Ted, as he and his sister watched their uncle and their aunt out in the big yard back of the house.

"Well, I call it a shack, though your aunt calls it a bungalow," was the answer. "Between us I guess we'll manage to make something in which you Curlytops can have fun. I've made 'em like this on the prairies—those are the big, wide plains, you know, out West, where there are very few trees, and not much lumber," he went on. "We have to use old boards, tree limbs, when we can find them, and anything else we come across.

"It used to be that way, though there is more lumber now. But I've often taken a few sticks and boards and made a sort of shelter and then covered it with snow. It will stand up almost all winter, if you don't let a goat knock it down," he added with a laugh.

"We won't let Nicknack knock this snow bungalow down," said Janet.

"No, we'll coax him to be good," added Aunt Jo.

It had stopped snowing, though heavy clouds overhead seemed to hold more that might fall down later, and the Curlytops had not given up hope of being snowed in, though really they did not know all the trouble that might be caused by such a thing.

There were plenty of boards and sticks in the Martin barn and around it, and Aunt Jo and Uncle Frank had soon made a framework for the bungalow. It was larger than the first snow house the children had made, and it was to have a wooden door to it so the cold could be kept out better than with a blanket.

"What are you doing?" asked Tom Taylor on Thanksgiving day morning, when he came over to play with Jan and Ted.

"Making a snow bungalow," Ted answered. "Want to help?"

"My, yes!" answered Tom. "Say, it's going to be a dandy!" he exclaimed when he had been introduced to Aunt Jo and Uncle Frank, and was told what they were doing to give the Curlytops a good time.

When the dinner-bell rang the wooden part of the bungalow was nearly finished and there were two windows in it of real glass, some old sashes having been found in the barn. These had once been in a chicken coop.

"Well, we're glad to have Uncle Frank and Aunt Jo with us for the Thanksgiving dinner," said Daddy Martin, as they all sat at the table.

"And I'm going to be right next to my dear little Trouble!" cried Aunt Jo, reaching over to hug Baby William.

"Look out he doesn't eat everything off your plate," warned Mother Martin with a laugh. "He says he's very hungry."

"Well, that's what everybody ought to be on Thanksgiving day," said Uncle Frank. "We ought to be hungry enough to like a good dinner, and be thankful we have it, and wish everybody else had the same."

"That's right!" cried Daddy Martin, and then he began to carve the big, roasted turkey, while Mother Martin dished out the red cranberry sauce.

I will not tell you all the good things there were to eat at the Martins' that Thanksgiving, for fear I might spoil your appetite for what you are going to have to-day—whatever day it happens to be. Not that you might not have just as nice a dinner, but it will be different, I know.

Such a brown, roasted turkey, such red cranberry sauce, such crisp, white celery and such a sweet pumpkin pie—never were they seen before—at least as far as I know.

There was eating and talking and laughter and more eating and more talking and more laughter and then they began all over again.

At last even Uncle Frank, who was a bigger man than Daddy Martin, said he had had enough to eat. So the chairs were pushed back, after

Nora had brought in some snow cream, which was something like ice cream only made with snow instead of ice, and Uncle Frank told about a prairie fire.

Then Aunt Jo told one about having been on a ship that struck a rock and sank. But no one was drowned, she was glad to be able to say.

Ted and Jan liked to listen to the stories, but they kept looking out in the back yard, and finally Uncle Frank said:

"I know what these Curlytops want!"

"What?" asked Mother Martin.

"They want to go out into the yard and finish the snow bungalow! Don't you, Curlytops?"

"Yes!" cried Jan and Ted.

"And I want to go out, too," went on Uncle Frank, "for I'm not used to staying in the house so much, especially after I've eaten such a big dinner. So come on out and we'll have some fun."

"I'm coming, too!" cried Aunt Jo. "I love it in the fresh air and the snow."

"Come on, Mother Martin!" called Mr. Martin to his wife. "We'll go out with them. It will do us good to frolic in the snow."

"All right. Wait until I get on some rubbers."

"Me come, too!" cried Trouble, who had fallen asleep after dinner, but who was now awake.

"Yes, bring him along," said Daddy Martin.

They were soon all out in the yard. The storm had not started in again, but Uncle Frank said it might before night, and there would, very likely, be much more snow.

Then they began the finishing touches on the snow bungalow. They piled the masses of white flakes on top of and on all sides of the board shack, or cabin, Uncle Frank and Aunt Jo had built. Soon none of the boards, except those where the door was fastened on, could be seen. They were covered with snow.

"There!" cried Uncle Frank, when the last shovelful had been tossed on. "There's as fine a snow bungalow as you could want. It will be nice and warm, too, even on a cold day."

"And Nicknack can't knock it down, either," added Ted.

"Well, he'll have harder work than he did to knock down the plain snow house you built," said Aunt Jo. "Now let's go inside and see how much room there is."

The bungalow would not hold them all at once, but they took turns going in, and it was high enough for Uncle Frank to stand in, though he had to stoop a little.

Some benches and chairs were made of the pieces of wood left over and Uncle Frank even built a little table in the middle of the play bungalow.

"You can eat your dinners here when it's too warm in the house," he said with a laugh.

Then Ted, Janet, Tom Taylor and his sister Lola had fun in the new bungalow while the older folk went in to sit and talk of the days when they were children and played in the snow.

Daddy Martin told about the strange lame boy who had come to his store and, later, to the house, but who had gone away without waiting to tell what he wanted.

"Ted and Jan are anxious to see him to make sure he is not their friend Hal," said Mr. Martin. "But I do not think it is. Hal would not take a pocketbook."

"Then you have never found the lost money?" asked Mrs. Martin.

"No, never," her husband answered. "Still I do not want to say the lame boy took it until I am more sure."

The Curlytops and their friends played in the yard around the snow bungalow until it was getting dark. Trouble had been brought in some time before by his mother, and now it was the hour for Jan and Ted to come in.

"We'll go coasting to-morrow, Tom!" called Ted to his chum.

"All right," was the answer. "I'll call for you right after breakfast."

"We'll hitch Nicknack to the big sled and make him pull us to the hill," said Janet, for Mr. Martin had bought a large, second-hand sled to which the goat could be harnessed. The sled would hold five children, with a little squeezing, and Trouble was often taken for a ride with his brother and sister, Tom and Lola also being invited.

"Come to supper, children!" called Mrs. Martin, as Ted and Jan came in from having spent most of the afternoon in the snow bungalow. "I don't suppose you are hungry after the big dinner you ate," she went on, "but maybe you can eat a little."

"I can eat a lot!" cried Ted.

"I'm hungry, too," added Janet.

"Well, I wish you'd wash Trouble's hands and face, Jan," went on Mrs. Martin. "I hope you didn't let him throw too many snowballs."

"Why, Trouble wasn't with us—not after you brought him in!" exclaimed Ted.

"He wasn't?" gasped Mrs. Martin. "Hasn't he been out with you since about an hour ago, and didn't he come in with you just now?"

"No," answered Jan.

"Why, I put on his mittens, little boots and jacket," said his mother, a worried look coming over her face. "He said he wanted to go out and play with you. I opened the back door for him, and just then Aunt Jo called me. Are you sure he didn't go out to you?"

"No, he didn't," declared Jan. "We haven't seen him since you brought him in. Oh, dear! is Trouble lost?"

Mrs. Martin set down a dish that was in her hand. Her face turned pale and she looked around the room. No Trouble was in sight.

"What's the matter?" asked Mr. Martin, coming in just then.

"Why, I thought Baby William was out in the yard, playing with Jan and Ted," said Mrs. Martin, "but they came in just now and they say he wasn't. Oh, where could he have gone?"

"Maybe he went out in the front instead of to the back when you put on his things," said Aunt Jo, "and he may be in one of the neighbor's houses. We'll go and ask, Uncle Frank and I."

"I'll come, too," said Mr. Martin. "Mother, you call through the house. He may not have gone out at all."

CHAPTER XIII
NICKNACK HAS A RIDE

MRS. MARTIN hurried into the hall and in a loud voice called:

"Trouble! Trouble! Where are you? Baby William! Come to Mother!"

There was no answer. Ted and Jan looked anxiously at each other. Their father had gone with Uncle Frank and Aunt Jo to inquire in the houses next door and those across the street. Sometimes Trouble wandered to the neighbors', but this was in the summer, when doors were open and he could easily get out. He had never before been known to run away in winter.

"Oh, where can he be?" exclaimed Janet.

"We'll find him," declared Teddy.

He saw that Janet was almost ready to cry.

"Help me look, children," said Mrs. Martin. "He may be in one of the rooms here. We must look in every one."

So the search began.

The Curlytops and their mother had gone through about half the rooms of the house without finding Trouble when Uncle Frank and Aunt Jo came back.

"Did you find him?" they asked Baby William's mother.

"No," she answered. Then she asked eagerly: "Did you?"

"He hadn't been to any of the neighbors' houses where we inquired," said Uncle Frank.

"Dick is going to ask farther down," added Aunt Jo. "I think he said at a house where a little boy named Henry lives."

"Oh, yes! Henry Simpson!" exclaimed Ted. "Trouble likes him. But Henry's house is away down at the end of the street."

"Well, sometimes William goes a good way off," said his mother. "I hope he's there. But we must search all over the house."

"And even down cellar," added Uncle Frank. "I know when I was a little fellow I ran away and hid, and they found me an hour or so later in the coal bin. At least so I've been told. I don't remember about it myself. I must have been pretty dirty."

"Oh, I don't think Trouble would go in the coal," said his mother. "But, Nora, you might look down there. We'll go upstairs now."

With Uncle Frank and Aunt Jo to help in the search the Curlytops and their mother went up toward the top of the house. Mother Martin looked in her room, where Trouble slept. He might have crawled into her bed or into his own little crib, she thought. But he was not there.

"He isn't in my room!" called Ted, after he had looked about it.

"Are you sure?" asked the anxious mother.

"Yes'm."

"And he isn't here," added Janet, as she came out of her room. "I looked under the bed and everywhere."

"In the closet?" asked Uncle Frank.

"Yes, in the closet, too," replied Janet.

"Maybe he's in my room," said Aunt Jo. "It's a large one and there are two closets there. Poor little fellow, maybe he's crying his eyes out."

"If he was crying we'd hear him," remarked Ted.

He and Janet followed Aunt Jo into her room. The light was turned on and they looked around. Trouble was not in sight and Aunt Jo was just starting to look in her large clothes closet when she suddenly saw something that caused her to stop and to cry out:

"Oh, what made it move?"

"What move?" asked Uncle Frank, who had followed her and the Curlytops in. "What did you see move?"

"My big suitcase," replied Aunt Jo. "See, it's there against the wall, but I'm sure I saw it move."

"Did any of you touch it?" asked Uncle Frank.

"No," answered Aunt Jo; and Ted and Jan said the same thing.

"What is it?" Mother Martin asked, coming into the room. "Did you find him?" she asked anxiously. "He isn't in my room, nor in Ted's or Janet's. Oh, where can he be?"

"Look! It's moving again!" cried Aunt Jo.

She pointed to the suitcase. It was an extra large one, holding almost as much as a trunk, and it stood against the wall of her room.

As they looked they all saw the cover raised a little, and then the whole suitcase seemed to move slightly.

"Maybe it's Skyrocket, our dog," said Ted. "He likes to crawl into places like that to sleep."

"Or maybe it's Turnover, our cat," added Janet.

Uncle Frank hurried across the room to the suitcase. Before he could reach it the cover was suddenly tossed back and there, curled up inside, where he had been sleeping, was the lost Trouble!

"Oh, Trouble, what a fright you gave us!" cried his mother.

"Were you there all the while?" Aunt Jo demanded.

Trouble sat up in the suitcase, which was plenty big enough for him when it was empty. He rubbed his eyes and smiled at those gathered around him.

"Iss. I been s'eepin' here long time," he said.

"Well, of all things!" cried Aunt Jo. "I couldn't imagine what made the suitcase move, and there it was Trouble wiggling in his sleep."

The Curlytops Snowed In

"How did you come to get into it?" asked Uncle Frank.

"Nice place. I like it," was all the reason Trouble could give.

He still had on his jacket and rubber boots which his mother had put on him when he said he wanted to go out and play in the snow with Jan and Ted.

"And, instead of doing that he must have come upstairs when I wasn't looking and crawled in here," said Mrs. Martin. "You mustn't do such a thing again, Baby William."

"Iss, I not do it. I'se hungry!"

"No wonder! It's past his supper time!" cried Aunt Jo.

"Did you find him?" called the anxious voice of Daddy Martin from the front door. He had just come in. "He wasn't down at the Simpsons'," he went on.

"He's here all right!" answered Uncle Frank, for Mrs. Martin was hugging Trouble so hard that she could not answer. She had really been very much frightened about the little lost boy.

"Well, he certainly is a little tyke!" said Mr. Martin, when he had been told what had happened. "Hiding in a suitcase! That's a new kind of trouble!"

They were all laughing now, though they had been frightened. Trouble told, in his own way, how, wandering upstairs, he had seen Aunt Jo's big suitcase, and he wanted to see what it would be like to lie down in it. He could do it, by curling up, and he was so comfortable once he had pulled the cover down, that he fell asleep.

The cover had not closed tightly, so there was left an opening through which Trouble could get air to breathe. So he did not suffer from being lost, though he frightened the whole household.

Supper over, they sat and talked about what had happened that day, from building the snow bungalow to hunting for Trouble. Before that part had been reached Trouble was sound asleep in his mother's lap, and was carried off to his real bed this time. A little later the

Curlytops followed, ready to get up early the next day to have more fun.

"Well, we haven't got that big storm yet, but it's coming," said Uncle Frank, as he looked at the sky, which was filled with clouds.

"And will we be snowed in?" asked Ted.

"Well, I wouldn't exactly say that," his uncle answered. "Would you like to be?"

"If you and Aunt Jo will stay."

"Well, I guess we'll have to stay if we get snowed in, Curlytop. But we'll have to wait and see what happens. Where are you going now?"

"Over on the little hill to coast. Want to come with me, Uncle Frank?"

"No, thank you. I'm too old for that. I'll come some time, though, and watch you and Janet. What are you going to do with your goat?" he asked, as he saw Ted taking Nicknack out of the stable.

"Oh, our goat pulls us over to the hill in the big sled, and then we slide down hill on our little sleds. I'm going to take Jan and Tom Taylor and Lola."

"And Trouble, too?" Uncle Frank asked.

"Not now. Trouble is getting washed and he can't come out."

"No, I guess he'd get cold if he did," laughed Uncle Frank.

He helped Ted hitch Nicknack to the big sled, not that Ted needed any help, for he often harnessed the goat himself, but Uncle Frank liked to do this. Then the Curlytops and Tom and Lola Taylor started for the hill.

There they found many of their playmates, and after Nicknack had been unhitched so he could rest he was tied to a tree and a little hay put in front of him to eat. The hay had been brought from home in the big sled which stood near the tree to which Nicknack was tied, and Ted and Jan began to have fun.

101

Down the hill they coasted, having races with their chums, now and then falling off their sleds and rolling half way down the hill.

"I know what let's do, Teddy," said Jan after a bit.

"I know something, too!" he laughed. "I can wash your face!"

"No, please don't!" she begged, holding her mittened hands in front of her. "I'm cold now."

"Well, it'll make your cheeks nice and red," went on Teddy.

"They're as red now as I want 'em," answered Jan. "What I say let's do is to see can go the farthest on our sleds."

"Oh, you mean have a race?"

"No, not zactly a *race*," answered the little girl. "When you race you see who can go the *fastest*. But now let's see who can go the *longest*."

"Oh, I see!" exclaimed Teddy. "That will be fun. Come on!" and he started to drag his sled to the top of the hill, Janet following after, "like Jack and Jill," as she laughingly told her brother.

When the two children were about half way up the hill, their heads bowed down, for the wind cut into their faces, they heard a shout of:

"Look out the way! Look out the way! Here we come!"

Ted and Jan looked up quickly and saw, coasting toward them, another little boy and girl on their sleds.

"Come over here!" cried Teddy to his sister. "Come over on my side of the hill and you'll be out of the way."

"No, you come over with me!" said Janet. "This is the right side, and mother said we must always keep to the right no matter if we walked up or slid down hill."

"Well, maybe that's so," agreed Teddy. "I guess I'll come over by you," and he started to move across the hill, while the little boy and girl coasting toward him and Jan kept crying:

"Look out the way! Look out the way! Here we come!"

And then a funny thing happened. Teddy thought he was getting safely out of the way, and he certainly tried hard enough, but before he could reach the side of his sister Janet, along came the sled of the little boy, and right into Teddy's fat legs it ran.

The little boy tried to steer out of the way, but he was too late, and the next Teddy knew, he was sitting partly on the little boy and partly on the sled, sliding down the hill up which he had been walking a little while before.

"Oh!" grunted the little boy when Teddy part way sat down on him.

"Oh!" grunted Teddy.

The reason they both grunted was because their breaths were jolted out of them. But they were not hurt, and when the sled with the two boys on it kept on sliding downhill all the other boys and girls laughed to see the funny sight.

"Well!" cried Teddy when he reached the bottom of the hill and got up, "I didn't know I was going to have that ride."

"Neither did I," said the little boy, whose name was Wilson Decker. "Me and my sister were having a race," he went on, "and now she beat me."

"I'm sorry," said Teddy. "I didn't mean to get in your way. My sister and I are going to have a race, too, and that's what we were walking up to do when I sat on you. Don't you want to race with us? We're going to have a new kind."

"What kind, Curlytop?" the little boy asked.

"To see who can go the longest but not the fastest," answered Teddy. "Come on, it'll be a lot of fun!"

So the little boy and his sister, whose sled, with her on it, had first gotten to the bottom of the hill, went up together with Teddy, to where Jan was waiting for him.

"Oh, Teddy!" cried the little Curlytop girl, laughing, "you did look *so* funny!"

"I—I sort of *felt* funny!" replied Teddy. "They're going to race with us," he went on, as he pointed to Wilson Decker and his sister.

"That'll be nice," returned Janet. "Now we'll all get on our sleds in a line at the top of the hill. It doesn't matter who goes first or last, but we must start even, and the one who makes his sled go the longest way to the bottom of the hill beats the race."

They all said this would be fair, and some of the other children gathered at the top of the hill to watch the race, which was different from the others.

"All ready! I'm going to start!" cried Janet, and away she went, coasting down the hill. The other three waited a little, for there was no hurry, and then, one after the other, Wilson, Teddy and Elsie (who was Wilson's sister) started down the hill.

Janet's sled was the first to stop at the bottom, as she had been the first to start, and she cried:

"Nobody can come up to me!"

But Elsie on her sled was exactly even with Janet.

"Well, if Teddy or your brother don't go farther than we did then we win the race—a half of it to each of us," said Janet.

And that's just what happened. Teddy's sled went a little farther than did Wilson's, but neither of the boys could come up to the girls, so Jan and Elsie won, and they were proud of it. Then they started another race.

They were having grand fun, shouting and laughing, when suddenly a strange dog, which none of the children remembered having seen before, ran along and began barking at Nicknack.

The goat, who was used to the gentle barking of Skyrocket, did not like this strange, savage dog, which seemed ready to bite him.

104

"Baa-a-a-a!" bleated the goat.

"Bow-w-w!" barked the dog, and he snapped at Nicknack's legs.

This was more than the goat could stand. With another frightened leap he gave a jump that broke the strap by which he was tied to the tree. Then Nicknack jumped again, and this time, strangely enough, he landed right inside the sled which, a little while before, he had pulled along the snow to the hill.

Right into the sled leaped Nicknack, and then another funny thing happened.

The sled was on the edge of the hill, and when the goat jumped into it he gave it such a sudden push that it began sliding downhill. Right down the hill slid the sled and Nicknack was in it.

"Oh, your goat's having a ride! Your goat's having a ride!" cried the other children to the Curlytops.

CHAPTER XIV
SNOWED IN

NICKNACK was indeed having a ride. Whether he knew it or not, or whether he wanted it or not, he was sliding downhill in the very sled in which he had pulled the Curlytops a little while before.

"Oh, look!" cried Janet.

"You'd better catch him 'fore he gets hurt!" added Tom.

"I never knew a goat could ride downhill!" laughed Jack Turton, a funny, fat, little fellow.

"Did you teach him that trick, Curlytop?" asked Ford Henderson, the big boy who had carried Janet home the day she went through the ice.

"I guess he must have learned it himself," answered Ted.

"That bad dog made him do it," said Janet. "Go on away, you bad dog!" she cried, stamping her foot.

Then Janet caught up some snow in her hand and threw it at the dog, which gave a surprised bark and ran away, with his tail between his legs, the way dogs do when they know they have done something wrong for which they deserve a whipping.

Perhaps, too, this dog was so surprised at seeing a goat ride downhill that he ran away on that account, and not because Janet threw a snowball at him. For a goat riding down a snow hill in a sled is certainly a funny sight. I never saw one myself, though I have seen a goat in a circus ride down a wooden hill made of planks and this goat sat on a seat in a wagon that, afterward, he drew about the ring with a clown in it.

So, I suppose, if a goat can ride downhill in a wagon it is not much harder to do the same thing in a sled.

At any rate, Nicknack rode down the hill, and the big sled kept going faster and faster as it glided over the slippery snow.

"Get out, Nicknack! Get out!" cried Janet, as she saw what was happening to her pet. "You'll be hurt! Jump out of the sled!"

Ted ran down the hill after the sliding sled, but as it was now going very fast, the little boy could not catch up to it.

"I guess your goat won't be hurt," said Ford Henderson to Jan. "Goats can climb rocks and jump down off them, so I guess even if his sled upsets and spills him out Nicknack won't get hurt."

"The snow is soft," said Lola.

"Look, he *is* going to upset!" cried Ted, who had stopped running and, with the other children, was looking down the hill. Nicknack was half way to the bottom now.

Just as Ted spoke the sled gave a twist to one side and Nicknack cried:

"Baa-a-a-a!"

Then, just as the goat was about to leap out, the sled ran into a bank of snow, turned over on the side and the next moment Nicknack went flying, head first, into a big, white drift.

"Oh, our nice goat will be killed!" cried Jan. "Oh, Teddy, you'd better go for a doctor!"

"No, Nicknack won't be hurt!" said Ford Henderson, the big boy, trying not to laugh, though Jan did make a very funny face, half crying. "Goats often land head first on their horns. Anyhow, I've read in a book that they do, and they don't get hurt at all. Goats like to fall that way. He's all right. See! He's getting out of the drift now."

And so Nicknack was. He had not been in the least hurt when he jumped, or was thrown, head first into the soft snow, though he might have broken one of his legs if he had rolled downhill with the sled. For that is what the sled did after it upset.

Kicking and scrambling his way out of the snow bank, Nicknack climbed up the hill again. He could easily do this, even without the pieces of rubber tied on his hoofs, for they were sharp hoofs, and he could dig them in the soft snow, as boys stick their skates into the ice.

Up came Nicknack, and then with a little waggle of his funny, short, stubby tail he walked over to a little hay still left near his feeding place, and began to eat.

"Say, he's a good goat all right!" cried Tom Taylor. "He's a regular trick goat! He ought to be in a circus."

"Maybe we'll get up a circus and have him in it some day next summer," promised Ted.

"You'd better go an' get our sled 'fore it's broke," called Janet to him.

"That's right," agreed Ford. "Some of the coasters might run into it and break it, or hurt themselves. I'll get it for you."

Ford was not coasting on the little hill, being too big a boy. But he liked the Curlytops and was always helping them when he could, even before he helped get Janet out of the frozen pond when she broke through the ice.

The heavy sled, to which Nicknack could be hitched, was not easy to pull up the hill, but Ford managed to do it. Then, after Ted, his sister and their playmates had coasted all they wanted to, the goat was harnessed again, and back home he trotted over the snow, pulling the Curlytops.

Ted had fastened some sleighbells to his pet, and they now made a merry jingle as Nicknack trotted along. The goat went quite fast, for I suppose he knew a nice supper of the things he liked was waiting for him in his stable. And it was not altogether pieces of paper off tin cans, either, though some goats like to chew that paper because it has sweet paste on it.

"Well, did you have a nice time?" asked Uncle Frank, as the Curlytops came home.

"Fine!" cried Janet.

"And Nicknack had a ride downhill!" added her brother.

"No!" exclaimed Uncle Frank, in surprise. "Now you're fooling me!"

"Nope!" said Ted earnestly. "He did, honest!" and he told all about it.

Aunt Jo and the other grown-ups also had to hear the story, and there was many a good laugh as the little Curlytops and the grown folks sat in the living-room that evening and talked over the things which had happened during the day.

"It's getting colder," remarked Daddy Martin, as he went out on the porch to look at the thermometer before going to bed.

"Does it look as if it would snow?" asked his wife.

"Well, there are no stars out, so it must be cloudy, and cloudy weather in winter generally means snow."

"Have we any of the roast turkey left from Thanksgiving?" asked Uncle Frank.

"Oh, yes, plenty," answered Daddy Martin. "Why do you ask?"

"Well, so if we get snowed in we'll have plenty to eat."

"Oh, we'll have plenty besides turkey," put in Mother Martin. "But I don't believe we'll get snowed in."

It was not quite time for Ted and Janet to go to bed, and they liked to sit up and listen to what their father and mother, Aunt Jo and Uncle Frank had to say. The Curlytops loved company as much as you children do.

Trouble had been put to bed, though not before he had made his sister and brother tell, over and over again, how Nicknack rode downhill on the sled. Trouble laughed each time he heard the story.

The Curlytops were playing a little game with Uncle Frank, and Aunt Jo, Daddy and Mother Martin were talking about the good times they used to have in winter when they were children, when Mrs. Martin said:

"I feel a cold wind blowing, don't the rest of you?"

"It is chilly," agreed her husband. "The wind must have sprung up suddenly and is coming through the cracks of the windows."

"There's more wind than comes through a crack," said Mrs. Martin. "I think a door is open. It comes from the front. Did you shut the hall door, Dick?"

"Yes, I closed it after I came in from looking at the thermometer," answered her husband.

"Well, I'm going to see what makes such a draft on my back!" exclaimed Mrs. Martin, getting up.

She went out into the hall, and the others did not think much more about it for a little while until Mrs. Martin suddenly cried:

"No wonder I felt a cold wind! Trouble Martin! What will you do next? Oh, dear! You're always doing something! Come in this instant!"

"What's he doing now? I thought he was safe in bed and away over in Dreamland," said Daddy Martin.

"So did I," returned his wife. "But he must have gotten up and come downstairs. I didn't hear a sound, but here the little tyke has the front door open! Oh, how cold it is!"

"What made you do it, Trouble?" his father asked, as he caught the little fellow up in his arms.

"Trouble want to see snow," was the answer.

"It is snowing, and snowing hard!" exclaimed Ted. "Hurray, it's a regular blizzard!"

Indeed it was snowing hard. Those inside had a glimpse of the storm before Daddy Martin closed the door Trouble had opened. It had not been fastened tight and the little boy had managed to pull it open.

He had awakened after being put to sleep for the night in his crib, and had crept downstairs. His mother thought the wind blowing the hard flakes of snow against a window near him must have awakened him.

"I'll go up to bed with him now," she said, "and I'll see that he doesn't get up again until morning."

"I guess we'll all go to bed," said Aunt Jo. "I'm tired and sleepy myself."

Ted and Jan looked out of the window as they began to undress.

"It's snowing hard," said Teddy.

"And maybe we'll be snowed in!" added his sister.

All night the storm raged. The wind blew hard and the snow came down in great, white feathery piles. Ted and Jan slept soundly, for they had played hard the day before. It was late in the day when they awakened, and they saw a light in the hall outside their room.

"What's the matter?" asked Janet, as she saw her mother up and dressed. "What you dressed for at night, Mother?"

"Hush! Don't wake Trouble. He was restless all night, but he is sleeping now. It isn't night, it's morning."

"But what makes it so dark?" asked Teddy.

"Because the snow covers nearly all the windows, especially on this side of the house."

"Is it snowing yet?" asked Jan.

"Yes; snowing hard," her mother answered.

"Are we snowed in?" asked Ted.

"Yes," replied Mrs. Martin, "I'm afraid we are snowed in, Teddy boy. It's a terrible storm, and very cold!"

CHAPTER XV
DRIVEN BACK

TEDDY and Janet, who had put on their bath robes as they crawled out of bed, looked at one another in the light that streamed into their mother's room from the hall. Their faces were happy. They were not afraid of the big storm. It was just what they had hoped would happen. But they did not know all the trouble that it was to cause.

"Are we really snowed in?" asked Janet.

"Yes, I think we really are," answered her mother, motioning to the children to come out into the hall so they would not awaken Trouble.

"Just like that hermit grandpa wrote about said we'd be?" Ted wanted to know.

"Well, I don't know just how big a storm that hermit thought would come," said Mrs. Martin; "but this is certainly a bad one. If you get dressed you can look out of the windows at the back of the house. The snow isn't so high there, and you can see what a lot has fallen in the night."

"Where's daddy?" asked Ted.

"He's getting ready to go out to the barn to see if the horse and cow are all right." The Martins had lately bought a cow, and they had had a horse for some time, though the children would rather ride behind their goat Nicknack than in the carriage with old Jim, who was not a very fast horse.

"Come on, Jan!" called Ted. "We'll get dressed and we'll go out and have some fun."

"Oh, no, you can't go out!" exclaimed his mother. "And please don't make much noise."

"Why can't we go out?" asked Janet at once.

"Because the snow is too deep. It's over your heads in some of the drifts, and it's so cold and still snowing so hard that I wouldn't dream of letting you Curlytops go out."

"Not even with our new rubber boots?" Teddy asked. "They are good and high and we could wade through the snow with them."

"Not even with your new rubber boots, Teddy boy. Now be good and don't tease. Get washed and dressed, and Nora will give you some breakfast."

"Come on!" called Ted in a whisper to his sister. "We'll have some fun anyhow! Snowed in! That's just what we wanted!"

"Snowed in, is it?" exclaimed Uncle Frank, coming from his room. "So you have got a real snowstorm here at last, have you?" he went on to Mrs. Martin. "Well, this makes me think of my ranch in the West. Where's Dick?" he asked.

"He's trying to see if he can get out to the barn to make sure the horse and cow have water and something to eat," said Mrs. Martin, for her husband had gotten up a little earlier.

"Well, I'll go and help him," said Uncle Frank. "I'm used to storms like this. It's a regular blizzard by the sound of it."

Indeed the wind was howling around the corner of the house, and at times it seemed to blow so hard that the house shook. As yet Ted and Jan had not had a look outside, for the windows upstairs, from which they had tried to see the storm, were coated with snow. The window sills had drifted full of the white flakes, and more had been piled on top of them. Then the warmth inside the room had made the snow that blew on the windows melt a little. This had frozen and more snow had fallen and been blown on the glass until from some of the windows nothing at all could be seen.

"But if you go downstairs to the kitchen I think you can look out a little," said Mrs. Martin to her two Curlytops.

Downstairs hurried Janet and Teddy. They only stopped to call "Good-morning!" to Nora, who was busy at the stove, and then the two children pressed their faces against the window panes.

They could not see much at first—just a cloud of swirling snowflakes that seemed to fill the air to overflowing. Then Janet cried:

"Why, it's almost up to the window sill, Teddy!"

"That's right! The back yard is full of snow, Nora!"

"I know it is. I went in over my knees when I went out to see if the morning paper had come."

"Did it come, Nora?"

"Indeed it didn't! I guess there won't be any paper for a few days if this storm keeps up, for the boys can't get around to deliver it. I could hardly get the door shut after I opened it. It's terrible!"

"It's fun!" cried Teddy.

"Course it is!" agreed Janet. "We wanted to be snowed in!"

"Well, you got your wish, Curlytops, and I hope it isn't any worse than that," said Nora. "Though how we're to get out of the house and get things to eat is more than I know."

"We've got lots left from Thanksgiving," said Teddy.

"Haven't we got any milk?" asked Janet.

"Oh, yes, there's plenty left from last night, though if the storm keeps up I don't see how your father is going to get out to the barn to milk the cow, and Patrick cannot get over to do it through this storm."

Patrick was a man who milked for the Martins and sometimes did other work for them about the place.

"Daddy can milk," said Ted.

"Yes, I know he can," agreed Nora, "if he can only get out to the barn. But look at the big drifts in the yard."

Jan and Ted looked out again. The yard was indeed filled with great heaps of snow, many of them higher than the heads of the children. The yard was a big one and at the far end was the barn.

"Oh, look!" cried Ted. "Our snow bungalow is gone, Janet!"

"Oh, it's blowed down!" cried Janet.

"No, it hasn't," said Nora. "I could just see the tip top of it when I got up early this morning, but now the snow has covered it. The bungalow is there all right, but you can't see it. It's under a big drift."

"Oh, wouldn't it be fun if we were out in it now?" cried Teddy.

"Indeed, and you'd starve and freeze," laughed Nora.

"No, we wouldn't," declared Teddy. "It's nice and warm out there. Uncle Frank said he used to make snow bungalows like that out West and he's lived in one a whole week in a blizzard."

"But he had something to eat," went on Nora, "and there's nothing in your bungalow."

"Yes, there is, a little," remarked Teddy. "We had a play party in it yesterday—Jan, me and Trouble, and we left some of the things we couldn't eat. I put 'em in a box and tied 'em up in a piece of carpet we had there. I was going to come back and make-believe I was a tramp and awful hungry, only I forgot it. There's things to eat out there, Nora. We wouldn't starve."

"Well, I guess your mother wouldn't let you go out there and play anyhow, in this storm."

"We'll have some fun in the house," said Janet. "Oh, doesn't it snow, Ted!"

There came a big gust of wind just then and a cloud of snow hid the yard from sight. All the children could see was a lot of whiteness.

"Oh, what about Nicknack?" asked Jan suddenly.

"What you mean?" asked her brother.

"I mean will he have enough to eat? Maybe we've got to go out and feed him."

"I gave him something to eat last night," said Teddy, "and I left a big pail of water in his stable. I guess he'll be all right. Anyhow Daddy and Uncle Frank are going out to the barn and they can feed our goat."

Nicknack had a little stable, like a big dog house, built next to the main barn, of which it was a part, though he had his own little door to go in and out.

"Get your breakfasts, children, and then you can sit by the window and watch the storm," said Mrs. Martin, coming into the kitchen just then. "Trouble is waking up and I'll want you to help take care of him. You'll all have to stay in the house to-day and play quiet games."

"Let's go and look out the front windows," proposed Janet.

She and Ted ran through the hall to the parlor. But from those windows they could see nothing, for the glass was either so crusted with snow, or the drifts were really so high in front of the windows, that it was impossible to look out.

"It is an awful big storm!" cried Janet as she went back to the warm dining-room. Not much could be seen from those windows, either.

"Maybe it will stop in a little while," said Teddy, "and then we can go out and have a ride with Nicknack."

"Indeed, Nicknack would be buried deep in the snow over his head if you took him out," said Aunt Jo, as she came downstairs. "You Curlytops haven't an idea how bad this storm is. I never saw a worse one. We may be snowed in for a week!"

"Hurray!" cried Teddy.

"It'll be fun," added Janet.

As the children sat down to breakfast, the lights being turned on because it was so dark, though it was nearly nine o'clock, their father and Uncle Frank got dressed ready to go out to the barn.

The men had on their overcoats, caps and big rubber boots. On their hands were warm gloves and each one carried a snow shovel, which the Curlytops' father had brought up from the cellar.

"We're going to try to get out to the barn," said Mr. Martin. "I'm not sure the cow and horse have enough to eat."

"Oh, can't I come?" begged Teddy.

"And me, too!" added Janet.

"No, indeed, Curlytops!" cried Mr. Martin. "You'd be lost in the snow and maybe Uncle Frank and I couldn't dig you out again. Stay here until we come back."

The children hurriedly finished their breakfasts, and then ran to the kitchen windows to see their father and Uncle Frank try to dig their way to the barn. And the men really had to dig their way, for between the barn and the house the drifts were too deep to wade through. Many of them were over the heads of Daddy Martin.

The Curlytops could see little, as the snow was still blowing and drifting. Now and then they saw their father or their Uncle Frank for just a moment, but the men were so covered with the white flakes that they looked like snow men.

Finally there was a stamping of feet in the back entry, and when Nora opened the door there stood Uncle Frank and Daddy Martin. They were covered with snow and looked very tired.

"What's the matter?" asked Mrs. Martin. "Couldn't you get to the barn, Dick?"

"No, we were driven back," her husband answered. "It is a terrible storm, and very cold. We dug a path part way to the barn, but the wind blew the snow in it, filling it up as fast as we could dig it out. I guess we can't get to the barn. We surely are snowed in!"

CHAPTER XVI
DIGGING A TUNNEL

EVEN seeing their father and uncle so tired out from shoveling snow and from struggling with the storm did not make the Curlytops think how bad it was to be snowed in. They still thought it was going to be fun. And so, in a way, it was, I suppose. At any rate they had a warm house in which to stay and plenty of good things to eat.

"Well, what are you going to do?" asked Mrs. Martin of her husband as, standing in the entry, he brushed some of the snow off his boots with the broom.

"We'll have to try again," said Uncle Frank.

"Is it like your out-West blizzards, Uncle Frank?" asked Teddy.

"Yes, this is almost as bad as the ones we have out there," he said. "Only this isn't quite so cold."

"It's cold enough for me!" exclaimed Mr. Martin. "Here, Jan," he called to his little girl. "Just take hold of my nose, will you, my dear?"

"What for, Daddy?" asked the little girl.

"I want to see if it is still fast to my face," answered her father. "It got so cold when I was shoveling snow that I thought maybe it had frozen and dropped off."

Janet grasped her father's nose in her warm hands.

"Oh, it's awful cold!" she cried with a little shiver.

"I know it is!" laughed Mr. Martin. "That's what made me afraid it was going to drop off. I'm glad I still have it."

"Are you cold, too, Uncle Frank?" asked Teddy.

"A little, yes. But I shoveled hard at the snow and I'm warmer now."

"Take some hot coffee," said Mrs. Martin. "Nora will pour it out for you. No, Trouble! You mustn't do that!" she cried, as she saw Baby William crumbling a slice of bread into the pitcher of milk.

"What's he doing?" asked Aunt Jo.

"Goin' make a cake," the little fellow answered. "Make cake an' have p'ay party."

"Well, you can have a play party with something else," laughed his mother. "We can't let you waste milk that way when we can't tell when we'll get more if daddy can't get out to the barn to milk the cow."

She took the slice of bread away from William and set him down from the table to which he had climbed up in a chair.

"'Member the time he made a cake when we were camping with grandpa on Star Island?" asked Janet of Ted.

"I guess I do!" he laughed. "The dough was all over everything!"

"Well, let's try it again now," said Uncle Frank to Daddy Martin, when they had had some hot coffee. "We've got to get out to the barn, somehow."

"Yes," agreed the father of the Curlytops. "I don't want the horse and cow to be hungry or thirsty. I hope the water in the barn isn't frozen. If it is we'll have to carry some from the house."

"And that might freeze on the way out," said Uncle Frank.

"You could take a pail of hot water and that wouldn't freeze," Teddy remarked.

"Our horse or cow couldn't drink hot water," objected Janet.

"Well, they could wait for it to cool just as we do for our hot milk sometimes."

"Yes, they could do that," agreed Janet. "Oh, I wish we could go out in our bungalow!"

119

"Don't dare try it!" cried Daddy Martin. "If you children went out in the snow you might not get back until your ears and fingers were frost-bitten, to say the least."

"What does frost-bitten mean?" Teddy asked.

"Well, it means almost frozen," explained his mother. "Now you and Janet can take Trouble up to the playroom and have a good time, while I help Nora with the work."

"We want to see daddy and Uncle Frank dig in the snow out to the barn," said Teddy.

"Well, you may watch them a little while, and then take care of Baby William."

"You can't see very much," said Uncle Prank, "The snow is still coming down hard and it blows so we can hardly see one another. So you won't see much of us from the windows."

"Well, maybe we can see a little," remarked Janet, and she and Teddy, with Trouble between them, perched on chairs with their faces close against the snow covered glass. Of course the snow was on the outside, but it made the inside of the window-pane quite cold, and in a little while, Jan drew her face away and, feeling her nose, cried:

"Oh, Ted! It's frozen 'most, like daddy's was!"

"So's mine!" exclaimed Ted, feeling of his nose.

"Mine cold, too!" added Trouble, putting his chubby palm over his "smeller" as he sometimes called his nose.

Indeed the noses of the children were cold from having been pressed so long against the window, and when Aunt Jo heard what they had been doing she said:

"I wouldn't stay near the window any longer if I were you. The wind blows in a little, and it's drafty. You will get cold all over—not only your little noses. Go up to the playroom and I'll come, too. We'll have some fun."

"Just wait until we see if we can watch daddy and Uncle Frank a minute," pleaded Teddy.

They all looked out of the window again. Once in a while they had a glimpse of their father or his uncle tossing the snow to one side. The two men were trying to dig a path from the house to the barn, and they were down in a deep trench, with white walls on either side.

"This is a terrible storm!" said Aunt Jo as she went up to the playroom with the Curlytops and Trouble. "I hope no little boys or girls are out in it."

"I hope not, either," echoed Jan with a little shiver, as she heard the wind howl around the corner of the house and dash the hard flakes of snow up against the windows.

"If any boys or girls were out in it they could stay in our bungalow," said Ted. "There's some blankets in there and a little to eat."

"And they could drink snow for water," said Jan. "I ate some snow once and it tickled my throat."

"Snow isn't good to eat," said Aunt Jo. "Up near the North Pole, the Eskimos and travelers never eat snow. It would make them ill. They melt it and drink the water when they are thirsty. But I hope no little boy or girl has to leave his or her warm house and live in your bungalow, nice as it may be. I'm afraid they'd be pretty cold in it even with a blanket and a piece of carpet."

"If daddy and Uncle Frank would dig a path we could go out to our bungalow and see," observed Jan.

"Maybe there's a tramp in it, like we thought there was on Star Island," went on Ted.

And, though neither Ted nor Jan knew it, there was someone in their snow bungalow.

Up in the playroom the Curlytops and Trouble had fun with Aunt Jo. She told them stories and made up little games for them, while outside the storm raged and the snow came down faster than ever.

"Come on!" cried Teddy after waiting a bit, "let's play that guessing game some more."

"Oh, let's!" agreed Jan. "It's lots of fun!"

This was a game in which one of them would think of something in the attic—the old spinning wheel, the steamboat chair or maybe a string of sleigh bells. Then the one who had the turn of thinking would tell the others the first letter of the name of the thing thought of, and perhaps something about it. The others had to guess what it was, and whoever guessed first was next in turn to think of something.

Teddy, Jan and Aunt Jo played this game for a while, but it was not much fun for Trouble. He was too little to know how to spell the things he thought of, though he could name almost everything in the attic, even if he called some by nicknames he made up himself.

"Let's play something that will be fun for Trouble," said Aunt Jo after a while.

"What?" asked Teddy.

"How would hide the bean bag be?" asked Aunt Jo.

"We haven't any bean bag," replied Teddy. "We had one, but Trouble threw it in the hedge and we can't find it."

"Well, I can easily make one," said Aunt Jo, and this she quickly did, getting beans from the kitchen, and sewing a bag from a piece of cloth from the rag-bag.

"Now we'll let Trouble hide the bag first," said Aunt Jo, "as he hasn't had much fun this last hour. You take the bag of beans, Trouble dear, and hide it anywhere you like. Only you must remember where you put it, so when we give up, if we can't find it, you can get it to hide again."

"All right!" laughed the little fellow, and then they told him all over again so he would be sure and not forget.

"Maybe you look where I put it," said Trouble, when he was about to take the bag and hide it.

"No, well blind our eyes so we can't see," promised Jan.

"And we won't look until you tell us you're ready," added Ted.

"And I promise I won't peep!" laughed Aunt Jo.

"Aw wight!" said Trouble, with a wise look on his chubby little face.

Then the others closed their eyes, and turned their backs, so they would be sure to see nothing, and Trouble, with the bag of beans in his hand, went wandering about the attic looking for a place to hide what he hoped Aunt Jo and the others would have to look a long time for.

"Are you ready, Trouble?" asked Jan, after a bit.

"Have you hid it yet?" inquired Ted.

"Yes, I put it hid," answered Baby William, and when they looked they saw him sitting on the floor near the chimney.

Then began the hunt for the bean bag. Aunt Jo and the two Curlytops looked in all the places in which they thought Trouble might have hidden it. They peered into boxes and old trunks, under boards, around the ledges of rafters and beams and everywhere.

"I guess we can't find it!" said Aunt Jo at last. "You hid it too well, Trouble. Tell us where you put it and then hide it in an easier place next time. Where is the bean bag, dear?"

"I—I *sittin'* on it!" laughed Trouble, and when he got up, there, surely enough, was the bag under him on the attic floor.

How they both did laugh at him, and Trouble laughed, too, and they had lots more fun, each one taking a turn to hide the bag.

Now and then the children would go to the window to look out, but they could see little. All Cresco was snowed in. As far as the children could see, no one was in the street.

Cresco, where the Curlytops lived, was a large town, and there was a trolley line running through it, but not near the home of Janet and Ted.

"But I guess the trolley isn't running to-day," Teddy remarked, after a game of bean-bag.

"I guess not," agreed Aunt Jo. "The cars would be snowed under."

Just then Mrs. Martin called Aunt Jo to help her with some work, and the children were left to themselves. They ran to the window, hoping they could see something, but the snow was either too high on the sill or the glass was frosted with the frozen flakes so no one could look through.

"Let's open the window!" suddenly proposed Ted. "Then we can get a little snow and make snowballs and play with 'em in here."

"Oh, let's!" cried Janet.

"Me want snowball, too!"

"We'll give you a little one," promised his sister.

By standing on a chair Teddy managed to shove back the catch of the window, but to raise the sash was not so easy. It was frozen down, and held fast by the drift of snow on the sill.

"I know how to raise it," said Jan.

"How?" asked her brother.

"Get daddy's cane and push it up. I saw Aunt Jo do it the other day."

Mr. Martin's cane was down in the hall, and Ted soon brought it upstairs. He put one end of it under the upper edge of the lower window sash and then he and Jan pushed with all their might. But the window did not go up.

"Push harder!" cried Teddy.

"I am!" answered Janet.

They both shoved as hard as they could on the cane and then it suddenly slipped. There was a crash and a tinkle of glass, and the children toppled over on the floor while the room was filled with a swirl of snowflakes blown in through the broken window.

"Oh, it's busted!" cried Teddy. "You did it, Janet Martin!"

"Oh, The-o-dore Baradale Martin! I did not! You pushed it yourself!"

"I didn't!"

"You did so!"

"Well, who got the cane, anyhow?"

"Well, who told me to get it?"

"I got some snow! I got some snow!" cried Trouble, and he tossed handfuls at his brother and sister, who had risen to their feet and were looking at the broken glass. The end of the cane had gone through it and the wind and snow were blowing into the room. On the carpet was a white drift that had fallen from the window sill.

"Oh, children! what *are* you doing?" cried Mrs. Martin, when she saw what had happened.

"The window broke," said Teddy slowly.

"Yes, I see it did," answered his mother. "Who did it?"

Then Teddy proved himself a little hero, for he said:

"I—I guess I did. I got the cane and it slipped."

"I—I helped," bravely confessed Janet. "I told him to get the cane and I pushed on it, too."

"Well, I guess you didn't mean to," said Mrs. Martin kindly. "But it's too bad. We can't get the window fixed in this storm, and daddy will have to nail a board or something over the hole. Trouble, come away from that snow!"

Trouble was having fun with the snow that came in through the hole, and did not want to stop. But his mother caught him up in her arms and took him out of the room, sending in Nora to sweep up the pile of white flakes on the carpet.

Then Daddy Martin nailed a heavy blanket over the window to keep out the cold wind, though a little did come in, and snow also.

"Did you and Uncle Frank dig a path out to the barn?" asked Teddy, when the excitement over the broken window had died down.

"Not yet," answered his father. "I guess we'll have to make a tunnel."

"Oh, a real tunnel, like railroad trains go through?" cried Ted.

"Yes, only made of snow instead of earth and rocks. We're going to make a snow tunnel."

"Oh, that'll be fun!" exclaimed Jan.

CHAPTER XVII
IN A BIG DRIFT

"WHAT are you men going to do now?" asked Mrs. Martin, as her husband and Uncle Frank sat near the stove in the kitchen warming their feet, for they were very cold, having come in after a second attempt to make a path to the barn.

"We're going to try a tunnel," said Mr. Martin. "The snow is too deep between the back door and the barn to try to shovel a path through it. As fast as we toss the snow away it blows in again and fills up the path so we can hardly get back to the starting place. Now if we begin in front of the house, where there is a big drift, we can tunnel out to the side of the barn."

"What good will that do?" asked Aunt Jo.

"When we make a tunnel it will have a top on it, like a roof over a house. It will be a long snow house, the tunnel will, and the snow can't blow in and fill it up."

"But what will you do with the snow you dig out of the tunnel?" Mrs. Martin enquired. "You'll have to dig ahead and pile the snow back of you and you'll be just as badly off."

"No," said her husband. "In front of the house is a big drift that goes all the way to the barn. But one side of the drift, near the house, is low and we can make a hole there to start. Then as we dig away the snow we can bring it back to this hole and dump it outside. If we work long enough we'll have a tunnel right through to the barn."

"In what will you carry the snow out of the tunnel?" asked Aunt Jo.

"In the big clothes baskets," answered Daddy Martin. "A tunnel is the only way I can see by which we can get out to the barn. Come on, Uncle Frank! If your feet are warm enough we'll begin. The horse and cow will be glad to see us."

"Can't you make a place so the children can watch you?" asked Mother Martin. "I can't have them in the playroom now as the window is broken. Scrape off some snow around the front windows so they can see what you're doing."

"We will," promised Uncle Frank.

So before he and Daddy Martin began to dig the tunnel they made a cleared place in front of one of the parlor windows so a view could be had of the big drift where the tunnel was to be started.

"Oh, I wish I could dig!" cried Ted.

"So do I!" echoed Janet.

"Don't you Curlytops open any more windows, or try to get out where your father and Uncle Frank are making the tunnel," warned Mrs. Martin. "This storm is getting worse instead of stopping."

So the children stayed by the window and watched.

With their big, wooden shovels and the big clothes baskets in which to pile the snow they dug from the tunnel, Daddy Martin and Uncle Frank started off to their work.

As the children's father had said, there was a large drift near the front of the house. On one side it sloped sharply to the ground, making a sort of snow wall, almost straight up and down. It was in the middle of this snow wall that the tunnel hole was to be started.

"Well, here we go!" cried Uncle Frank, as he waved his shovel at the watching children in the window.

He made a jab into the snow wall, and cut out a big square chunk of whiteness. This he tossed back of him out of the way. For a time this could be done, and there was no need to use the baskets. But as the tunnel was dug farther in, the pile of white flakes would have to be carried out. As the tunnel was only going to be big enough for one person to walk in at a time, and not wide enough for two to go side by side, the two men were to take turns digging, one using the shovel and the other bringing out the clothes basket filled with snow which would be emptied outside.

"Oh, I can't see Uncle Frank any more!" cried Ted, who was eagerly watching with his sister and Trouble.

"Where's he gone?" asked Janet.

"He's dug a hole for himself inside the snow bank—in the tunnel— and I can't see him now. He's away inside! Oh, what fun! I wish we could be in there," he added.

"So do I," echoed Janet. "Maybe we can when it gets warmer and the snow stops coming down."

"We'll ask mother," decided Teddy.

"I see my papa!" suddenly called Trouble. "He's bringin' out de clothes!"

"No, that's a basket of snow he has," said Janet with a laugh, for her father had just then come out of the tunnel with the first load of snow that had been dug loose by Uncle Frank.

From then on, for some time, the children had a sight of their father or their Uncle Frank only once in a while, as either one or the other came to the mouth of the tunnel to empty the basket filled with snow. Sometimes it would be Daddy Martin and again Uncle Frank, as they were taking turns.

"I guess the tunnel must be most finished," said Janet, when they had been watching for some time.

"Anyhow here they come in," added Teddy, as he heard a noise at the back of the house.

"Did you tunnel your way to the barn?" asked Mrs. Martin, as her husband and Uncle Frank came into the kitchen.

"Not yet. It's farther than we thought, and hard work," answered Mr. Martin. "We came in to get some dinner and then we're going at it again."

"And will you see if Nicknack is all right when you get out to the barn?" asked Teddy.

"I surely will," promised his father. "I thought I heard him bleating when I first went out, so I guess he's all right."

"Couldn't you bring him into the house?" asked Janet.

"He's lonesome out there," added Ted.

"Bring your goat into the house?" cried Mother Martin. "Oh, my goodness, no!"

"Then we'd like to go out and see him," went on Teddy.

"Well, maybe, when we get the tunnel finished, and if it isn't too cold, I'll take you out," promised their father.

After dinner he and Uncle Frank began work on the tunnel again. The storm seemed to be stopping a little and the wind did not blow so hard.

"Please, Mother, couldn't Jan and I go out, just for a little while?" begged Teddy toward evening, when it was getting almost too dark for Mr. Martin and Uncle Frank to see to dig in the tunnel.

"What do you think, Aunt Jo?" asked Mrs. Martin.

"Oh, I should think it wouldn't hurt them to go out for a few minutes. Wrap them up well, and I'll go with them, on the side of the house where there isn't so much snow. But I wouldn't let Baby William go."

"No, I'll not."

So Ted and Jan and Aunt Jo got on their warm wraps and stepped out of the front door, where Daddy Martin and Uncle Frank had cleared a place on the veranda. Trouble cried to go, but, though the storm was not as bad as it had been at the start, it was too cold for him.

Ted and Janet did not mind it at first. They ran around, laughed, shouted and threw the snow. Then they began to feel the cold, which was more severe than they had thought.

"Oh, what big drifts!" cried Teddy, as he saw some out in the road.

"Awful big!" agreed Janet. "Let's go and look in the tunnel."

There was little to see, however, except a big white hole in the great drift, for Daddy Martin and Uncle Frank were at the far end, digging their way to the barn and Nicknack.

"Come now, it's time to go in," said Aunt Jo. "I promised your mother I'd keep you out only a little while. I think it's going to storm worse than ever. Come on in!"

"Please wait until I take one jump!" begged Teddy.

He gave a run and a jump, down a little side hill in the yard near the house. Into a pile of snow he leaped, and the next instant he had disappeared from sight! The snow had closed over his head!

"Oh, where is he? Where's Teddy?" cried Janet, very much frightened.

"I guess he's in the big drift!" answered Aunt Jo.

"Oh, Daddy! Uncle Frank!" cried Janet. "Come quick! Teddy's in a big drift!"

CHAPTER XVIII
NICKNACK IS GONE

DADDY MARTIN and Uncle Frank came running from the snow tunnel. Each one carried a shovel, for while the Curlytops' father had been digging away at the snow with his shovel, Uncle Frank had used the other to pile into the basket the loosened heap of white flakes.

"What's the matter?" asked Janet's father as he looked at her. "Why did you call me?"

"'Cause Teddy's in a big drift—down there!" she answered, pointing.

"Yes, he really did jump down there, and the snow was so soft that he went all the way through," added Aunt Jo.

"Then we must get him out in a hurry!" cried Uncle Frank. "Come on, Dick! This will be a new kind of digging for us."

"I should say so!" exclaimed Mr. Martin.

The two men ran toward the big drift, but when they got close they walked more carefully, for they did not want to make more snow fall in on top of Teddy through the hole he left when he jumped into the big drift.

"Are you down there, Son?" asked Mr. Martin, leaning over the hole and calling to the little boy.

Janet began to cry. She was afraid she would never see her brother again, and she loved him very much.

"Don't cry," said Uncle Frank kindly. "We'll get Teddy out all right. Did he answer you?" he inquired of Daddy Martin.

"Not yet, but I guess——"

Just then a voice seemed to call from under their very feet.

"Here I am!" it said. "Down in a big pile of snow. Say, can you get me out? Every time I wiggle more snow falls in on top of me!"

"We'll get you out all right, Ted!" shouted his father. "Just keep as still as you can. Can you breathe all right?"

"Yep!" came back the answer, as if from far away.

Then Daddy Martin and Uncle Frank began to dig in the big drifts with their shovels, while Aunt Jo and Janet looked on. As yet Mrs. Martin and Nora knew nothing about what had happened, nor did Trouble.

"But it's of no use to tell your mother and frighten her, Janet," said Aunt Jo. "They'll have Teddy dug out in a minute, and then he can tell her himself what happened to him, and we'll all have a good laugh over it."

"Won't he smother?" asked Janet.

"Oh, no," answered Aunt Jo. "Falling under snow isn't like falling under water. There is a little air in snow but not any in water—at least not any we can breathe, though a fish can. But still if a person was kept under heavily packed snow too long he would smother, I suppose. However, that won't happen to Teddy. They're getting to him."

Uncle Frank and Daddy Martin were tossing the snow away from the drift by big shovelfuls. In a little while they had dug down to where Teddy stood in a little hollow place he had scooped out for himself with his hands. He was covered with snow, but was not hurt, for falling in the big drift, he said, was like tumbling into a feather bed—the kind Trouble had once cut up when he was at his grandmother's on Cherry Farm.

"Well, how in the world did you get down there?" asked Teddy's father, when the little boy was lifted up safe on the path again, and the snow had mostly been brushed from him.

"I—I just jumped," Teddy answered. "I wanted to see how far I could go and I didn't think about that being the edge of the terrace."

For the big drift was on the edge of a terrace, where the front lawn was raised up from the rest of the yard. So the drift was deeper than any of the other piles of snow around it.

"However, you're not hurt as far as I can see," went on Mr. Martin. "But please don't go in any more drifts. Uncle Frank and I won't have time to dig you out, for we must keep at work on the tunnel."

"Isn't it finished yet?" asked Aunt Jo.

"No. And I don't believe it will be to-night. It's getting late now and we can't work much longer. It's going to snow more, too," added the father of the Curlytops as he looked up at the sky, from the gray clouds of which more white flakes were falling.

"Can't we go into the tunnel?" asked Teddy, who did not seem much frightened by what had happened to him.

"Well, yes, I s'pose you could go in a little way," his father answered. "We won't do any more digging to-night," he said to Uncle Frank.

"No, but we'd better put some boards in front of the hole we have dug to keep it from filling with snow in the night."

"Yes, we'll do that," said Mr. Martin.

The two men led the way to the tunnel, in which they had been digging most of the day. Aunt Jo, Teddy and Janet followed. At the window, one of the few out of which she could look into the big storm, Mrs. Martin motioned for the Curlytops to come in. Daddy waved his hand and called that he would bring them in as soon as he had showed them the tunnel.

The Curlytops thought this a wonderful place. They had been through railroad tunnels, but they were black and smoky. This snow tunnel was clean and white, not a speck of dirt being in it. Though it was cut through a great, white drift it was getting dark inside, for the sun was not shining, and night was coming.

"Wouldn't this be a dandy place to play?" cried Ted.

"Fine," answered Janet. "Nicer than our snow bungalow. When can we dig out to our bungalow?" she asked her father.

"Oh, in a day or two, I presume. It's pretty well covered with snow, and we must first see that the horse and cow are all right. It will be time enough to think of play after we have done that."

"And we've got to feed and water Nicknack, too," added Janet.

"Yes, we mustn't forget your goat," laughed Uncle Frank.

"Did you leave him any hay and water?" asked Daddy Martin.

"I did," Teddy answered. "I put a lot of hay where he could get it and some water to drink in a pail."

"Well, then maybe he'll have enough until we can dig our way out to him," said Mr. Martin. "But it isn't going to be easy. This has been a terrible storm, and I'm afraid it's going to be worse. I hope the poor of our town have coal enough to keep warm and enough food to eat. Being snowed in is no fun when one has to freeze and starve."

Teddy and Janet were glad they were so comfortable. They, too, hoped no one was suffering, and if they had known that not far away a poor boy was in great distress they would not have slept as well as they did that night. But they did not know until afterward, when they found out the secret about the snow bungalow.

"Well, come on out now," called Daddy Martin, as the Curlytops were looking at the snow tunnel. "It's time to go in. You've been out in the cold long enough."

"It is very cold," agreed Aunt Jo. "I'm just beginning to notice it."

Into the warm house they went, stamping and brushing off the snow that clung to them. As they gathered about the supper table, which was well filled with good things to eat, Nora came in to say that it was snowing again.

"I thought it would," remarked Daddy Martin. "We surely must finish that snow tunnel to-morrow," he said to Uncle Frank. "We may need the horse to help us break a way to the road."

"And we'll need more milk to-morrow," said Mother Martin.

That evening, as they sat in their warm house playing games and listening to the crackling of the corn which Aunt Jo popped, the Curlytops were very thankful for the nice home they had to stay in.

"How the wind blows!" cried Aunt Jo as she took the children up to bed.

"Is it snowing yet?" asked Teddy.

"I can't see," his aunt answered. "It's so dark and the snow covers the windows. But I wouldn't be surprised if it were. The storm is not over yet. I guess you children will have all the snow you want for once."

"We can have rides downhill for a long while," remarked Janet.

"And make snow men and snow forts and snowballs as much as we like," added Teddy.

All night long the storm raged again. The wind blew and the snow came down, but not as hard as it had the night before. If it had, there is no telling what would have happened. The Curlytops would have been snowed in worse than they were.

But it was bad enough, as they saw when they awakened and looked out the next morning. That is they tried to look out, but it was little indeed that they could see. For some of the windows from which they had had a glimpse of the outer world the day before were completely covered now.

"We'll have to do some digging to get to the opening of the tunnel," said Daddy Martin to Uncle Frank, "and we'll have to dig all day to get to the barn. But we've got to do it."

"That's right!" agreed Uncle Frank.

"Couldn't I help?" asked Teddy.

"No, I'm afraid not, Curlytop," answered his father. "It's pretty hard work for us men."

"But will you let me go out and see Nicknack as soon as you dig to his stable?" the little boy asked.

"I'll see about it—if the snow isn't too deep," his father replied.

"I want to come, too!" added Janet.

"Well, maybe you can," said Uncle Frank. "We'll see."

Then, after they had had a warm breakfast, the two men started the digging again. Teddy and Janet could not see them because they were so far inside the tunnel. And as the Curlytops could not be out to play they had to amuse themselves as best they could in the house.

Aunt Jo played with them and Trouble. Baby William was the hardest to amuse, as he was very active. He wanted to run about and do everything, and two or three times, when they looked for him, they found he had slipped away and was out in the kitchen, teasing Nora to let him make a cake.

It was well on in the afternoon when there came a stamping and pounding in the back entry.

"Oh, there's daddy and Uncle Frank knocking the snow off their feet!" exclaimed Janet.

"Maybe they've been out to the barn," said her brother.

"And maybe they've brought Nicknack in," added Janet.

The Curlytops ran to the kitchen, not stopping to wait for Trouble, who cried to be taken along. There in the entry, brushing the snow from them and stamping it from their boots, were Daddy Martin and Uncle Frank.

"Did you get to the barn?" inquired Teddy.

"Yes, we got there all right."

"And is our horse and cow all right?" Janet inquired.

"Yes, they're all right, and were glad to see us."

"Did you see our goat?" cried Teddy next.

"No, we haven't dug out to his stable yet. We're going to in a minute," said Daddy Martin.

"We thought we'd come in and get you two Curlytops and take you out to see Jim and the cow," added Uncle Frank.

"It isn't snowing quite as hard as it was, and it isn't quite so cold. We thought it might do the children good, for they've been cooped up all day," the children's father explained to his wife.

"So they have, but they haven't fretted much, except Trouble, and he didn't know any better. All right, take them out and then come in. We'll have an early supper. I do hope the storm will be over by to-morrow."

"I think it surely will," her husband said.

Teddy and Janet were soon warmly bundled up and were taken out of doors by their father and uncle. The keen wind cut their faces and the snowflakes blew in their eyes, but they liked it.

Through the snow tunnel they were carried to the barn door, which was open. It opened right into the snow tunnel, and inside was a lantern, for the barn was dark, being more than half covered with snow and there being only one or two windows in it.

Jim, the horse, whinnied when he heard his friends come in, and the cow mooed.

"They're glad to see us," said Janet.

"Yes, I guess they are," laughed her father. "I'm going to milk the cow. Then we'll shake down some hay for her and Jim, and give them more water, too. I'm glad the pump wasn't frozen."

So while Daddy Martin milked the cow, Uncle Frank tossed down hay from the mow upstairs in the barn and pumped some water.

"And now can't we get Nicknack?" asked Teddy, when a foaming pail of milk was ready to be carried to the house.

"Yes, I think so," answered his father.

"I called to him but he didn't answer," said Janet.

"I'll soon dig a way to Nicknack's place," said Uncle Frank, and he started at a point where the tunnel ran to the barn door. It did not take him long, with the big shovel, to clear a place so that the door to Nicknack's stable was free, for the drifts were not so deep on this side of the barn.

"Now for the goat!" cried Daddy Martin. "Stand back, Curlytops, and let Uncle Frank go first."

Uncle Frank, holding the lantern over his head, entered the goat's stable. He stood still for a few seconds.

"Is he all right?" asked Teddy anxiously.

"Well, I can't see him at all," Uncle Frank answered.

"You can't see him?" echoed Mr. Martin.

"No, Nicknack isn't here. He's gone!"

CHAPTER XIX
WHAT NICKNACK BROUGHT

TEDDY and Janet were so surprised they did not know what to say. They just stood and looked at one another in the light of the lantern their father held after having milked the cow. Uncle Frank was in Nicknack's little stable with another lantern.

"Are you sure he isn't there?" asked Mr. Martin, for well he knew how sorry the Curlytops would feel if anything happened to their goat.

"There isn't a sign of him," answered Uncle Frank. "You can come and look for yourselves."

"Maybe he's lying down asleep," suggested Teddy.

"I've looked all over," said Uncle Frank.

Teddy darted out of the barn, followed by Janet.

"Here! Come back!" cried their father. "You may get lost in the storm. It's snowing and the wind is blowing and it's hard to see where you're going, especially after dark."

"We want to see where Nicknack is," pleaded Teddy.

"Wait, and I'll go with you," his father remarked. "Perhaps he has burrowed down under the hay or straw to keep warm."

But when all four of them stood in front of Nicknack's little stable, which was too small for more than two to get in at a time, the Curlytops saw that their pet was not there. Uncle Frank flashed the lantern up high and down low, but no goat was to be seen.

"Where can he be?" asked Teddy, anxiously.

"Was the door fastened?" Daddy Martin inquired.

"Yes, it was shut and the catch was on. I had to take it off to get in," replied Uncle Frank. "Nicknack couldn't have gotten out that way."

"And there is only one door," went on Mr. Martin. "Did you look to see if any boards were loose on the sides of the stable, Uncle Frank?"

"No, I didn't, but I will."

With his lantern Uncle Frank began looking around the goat's stable, pushing against the boards, on the outside of which the snow was piled. Finally Uncle Frank gave a shout.

"What is it?" cried Teddy. "Have you found Nicknack?"

"No, but I've found the place where he got out. Look!"

Holding the lantern so all could see, Uncle Frank showed where a large board had been knocked loose. It swung to one side and showed a hole in the snow outside.

"Is he in there?" asked Jan, as she saw the hole. It was like the tunnel her father and Uncle Frank had dug, but smaller.

"I don't know whether he's there or not," answered Uncle Frank. "I'll have a look, though."

He pulled the board loose. It hung by one nail only. Then, stooping down so he could look into the hole, which seemed to have been dug in the snow outside, and flashing his lantern into it, Uncle Frank called:

"Here, Nicknack! Are you there? Come here!"

There was no answer, the only sound being the howl of the wind and the swish of the snowflakes in the storm.

"Isn't he there?" asked Teddy, his voice sounding as though he wanted to cry.

"I can't see him," answered Uncle Frank. "But I think he must be in the snow somewhere around here. We'll have to dig him out just as we dug you out of the big drift, Teddy."

"Is Nicknack in a drift?" Janet whispered. Somehow, if Nicknack were in a drift, it seemed better to Jan to talk in whisper.

"I can't imagine where else he would be," Uncle Frank said. "He must have gotten tired of staying here all alone, so, with his horns and head he just knocked this big board loose. That gave him room enough to get out, and then he began to dig his way through the snow. There was a little hollow place in the edge of the drift that is on this side of his stable, and that gave him a chance to start. He didn't paw any snow inside his stable, and that's why I didn't at first see which way he had gone."

"But how can we get him?" asked Jan, who felt the tears coming into her eyes.

"Oh, we can dig him out," her father said. "Don't worry. We'll soon get Nicknack for you."

"To-night?" Teddy demanded.

"Well, maybe not to-night," his father answered. "It's pretty late now, and getting colder. And there's no telling how far away Nicknack has dug himself into the snow bank. He's a strong goat, Nicknack is, and once he started to burrow through the snow, one couldn't say when he'd stop. He might even dig his way to the house."

"Honest and truly?" asked Teddy.

"Well, he might," said Mr. Martin. "Anyhow, we'll wait until morning before we start digging for him."

"But won't he die?" asked Janet.

"No, he can get air under the snow for quite a while, just as Teddy could when he jumped into the drift. And if he gets hungry he can wiggle his way back to his stable the same way he wiggled out. The way is open and we'll leave this board off so he can get in easily. There is hay and water here. The water didn't freeze, being warm under so much snow and down in the hay where you put the pail, Teddy. So Nicknack will be all right until morning I think."

"What made him go out?" asked Teddy.

"I think he got lonesome," laughed Uncle Frank. "He missed you two Curlytops, and he wanted to come to see you."

"But where is he?" asked Janet.

"Oh, somewhere in the snow between here and the house," answered her father. "Don't worry about Nicknack. He's able to take care of himself. Maybe he'll be back in his stable in the morning."

Janet and Teddy were not at all sure of this, but they hoped it might prove true. They liked their goat very much. He was a fine playfellow for them.

"Let us call, Jan," suggested Ted. "Nicknack likes us, and maybe he'll answer if we holler. You call first."

"All right," Jan responded. Then, at the top of her voice, she yelled: "Nicknack, come here!"

Then Teddy shouted: "Nicknack! Oh, Nicknack!"

Then they all waited in silence, but heard nothing in reply to their calls.

"Well, it's of no use to stay here any longer," said Daddy Martin, as they stood looking at Nicknack's empty stable. "We'll leave everything as it is and come here in the morning. It will be easy enough for us to get out, now that we have the tunnel made."

"Yes, come on back to the house, and I'll tell you some stories about my Western ranch," added Uncle Frank. "Some day I want you Curlytops to come out there and have pony rides."

"Oh, can we?" cried Teddy.

"To be sure you can."

"And shall we get snowed in?" asked Janet.

"Well, not if I can help it. But come in the summer when there won't be any snow. You'll like it out on my ranch in Montana."

The Curlytops were sure they would, and they were so anxious to hear more about it and talk of getting pony rides among the cowboys that, for the time, they forgot about Nicknack's trouble.

Back to the house they went, locking the stable door after seeing that the horse and the cow had plenty to eat. Daddy Martin carried the pail of milk, of which Trouble was to have his share, for he drank a great deal of it.

"Nicknack's gone!" cried Teddy as they entered the house, after brushing and shaking off the snow.

"Gone!" cried Mother Martin.

And then she and Aunt Jo were told what the Curlytops had discovered when they went to the goat's stable.

"Well, maybe he'll come back," said Aunt Jo. "After supper I'll tell you about a new bungalow I'm going to build at Ruby Lake, and I want you two Curlytops to come to see me there."

"Oh, won't we have fun at Uncle Frank's ranch and Aunt Jo's bungalow!" cried Teddy.

"Yes, we will!" echoed his sister.

After supper Uncle Frank began to tell a Western story of things that had happened at his ranch. He told of Indians having taken some of his ponies, and of how he and his cowboys chased and caught the Red-men and took back the little horses.

"We didn't want them to steal our ponies," he said.

"Daddy didn't want that lame boy to take the pocketbook in his store, but the lame boy did," said Janet, who was fast falling asleep.

"What made you think of that?" asked her father.

"Oh, I was just thinking," answered the little girl. "Maybe that lame boy was hungry like Uncle Frank said the Indians were."

"Maybe," agreed her mother. "But it isn't sure he took the pocketbook. You never found out who he was, did you?" she asked her husband.

"No, the poor fellow seemed to be too frightened to come back. I hope nothing happened to him. I'd rather lose the money than have him hurt, though, of course, I wouldn't want to learn that he would take what was not his. But now, Aunt Jo, it's your turn to tell about your new bungalow."

So Aunt Jo began her story, and by the time it was finished Teddy and Janet were ready for bed, where Trouble had gone long before.

"Still snowing," said Uncle Frank, as he went to the back door and looked out. "I imagine this is the biggest storm you folks in the East ever had."

"Yes, it is," agreed Daddy Martin.

The house was soon dark and quiet, while outside the cold wind blew and the snow piled in big drifts.

Janet and Teddy had fallen asleep, wondering what had happened to their pet goat, and the first thing they asked, on awakening in the morning was:

"Is Nicknack here?"

"We haven't seen him," answered their mother. "But daddy and Uncle Frank are going to dig for him after breakfast."

When the meal had been finished it was found that the snow had stopped, at least for a time, and that the weather was a little warmer. Janet and Ted were allowed to play out in a cleared place in the yard.

"Part of the tunnel caved in during the night," said their father, "and we'll have to dig it out before we can get to Nicknack's stable. But we'll call you as soon as we find him."

It took some time to dig through the snow, and while their father and Uncle Frank were doing this Ted and Janet made a little hill in the yard and slid down that on their sleds.

Then they saw Uncle Frank coming toward them.

"Did you find Nicknack?" called the Curlytops.

"No. We dug through the hole he made in the snow, but it came to an end at your bungalow, and there's no sign of the goat."

"Maybe he's in our play bungalow," said Teddy.

"The door is closed," went on his uncle. "I'm afraid your goat is snowed under farther off. We're going to dig some more after dinner. But we'll find him."

Janet and Teddy were worried about Nicknack.

"Please dig hard for him!" begged Janet, as the two men started out with their shovels after dinner.

"We will," they promised.

Just as they were going out to the kitchen, to get their shovels which they had left in the back entry, there came a pounding in that very place as though some one were stamping snow off his boots.

"What's that?" asked Uncle Frank.

"Someone coming to see us—one of the neighbors perhaps," remarked Mr. Martin. "This is the first any of them have broken out after having been snowed in."

Once more the pounding noise sounded.

"Come in!" cried Uncle Frank, as he started toward the door.

"Baa-a-a-a!" came the answer.

"Nicknack!" cried Teddy and Janet joyously.

Uncle Frank threw open the door. There stood the goat, covered with snow, and stamping to get off as much as he could. Into the kitchen he walked as though he felt at home there, and Teddy and Janet began to hug him.

"Hold on there! Wait a minute!" called their father.

"What is it?" asked Mrs. Martin. "What's the matter, Dick?"

"There's something on that goat's neck!"

"Something on his neck?"

146

"Yes, a note or something. Nicknack has brought in something out of the storm. We must see what it is!"

CHAPTER XX
IN THE BUNGALOW

THE Curlytops were very much excited when they heard their father say Nicknack had something on his neck. They had been so anxious to hug their pet that they had not thought of anything else, and had not noticed anything.

"We thought you were lost in the snow," murmured Janet.

"So he was," declared Teddy. "But he came in out of the snow," he added. "Didn't you, Nicknack?"

"Yes, and he brought something with him," went on Mr. Martin. "You must stop hugging Nicknack, Curlytops, until I see what it is."

He led the goat gently away from the children. Nicknack bleated again.

"I guess he's hungry," said Teddy.

"I'll get him a cookie!" offered Janet.

"You'd better give him a real meal," put in Nora. "He'll be hungry and want more than cookies, I'm thinkin'."

"Get him anything you like," said Mr. Martin, "as long as I get this off his neck. It is a note!" he cried. "It's tied on with a piece of string. It's a note—a letter!"

"Who in the world would send a note by Nicknack in that queer way, I wonder," remarked Mrs. Martin.

"I've read of persons lost in the mountains sending a note for help tied around the neck of a St. Bernard dog," said Uncle Frank. "Maybe somebody used Nicknack as a dog."

Meanwhile Teddy and Jan had to run to the pantry to get Nicknack something to eat. Trouble was now petting the goat and asking:

"Where you been, Nicknack? Where you been all dis while?"

"It is a note from some one in trouble!" cried Daddy Martin as he pulled the bit of paper from Nicknack's neck.

"What does it say?" asked Uncle Frank.

"And who is it from?" Mrs. Martin inquired.

"It's signed 'The Lame Boy,'" answered her husband. "And he must be in the snow bungalow the children built!"

"In the snow bungalow!" cried Aunt Jo in surprise.

"That's what it says. I'll read it to you," went on Mr. Martin. Then, while Teddy and Janet fed cabbage leaves and pieces of cookie to their goat, their father read aloud the short note.

"I am out in a little playhouse in your yard," the note read. "I hurt my foot so I can't walk and I am snowed in. This goat came in to see me and I tied this note on his neck. I thought maybe he would take it to somebody who would help me. I have only a little piece of bread left to eat. Please help me, whoever finds this."

"Help him! Of course we will!" cried Uncle Frank. "Where's my shovel? Come on, Dick! We've got to dig him out! Come on, everybody!"

"I want to help!" cried Teddy.

"So do I!" added Janet.

"Let me dig!" begged Aunt Jo. "I can handle a snow shovel as good as a man, and you must be tired, Uncle Frank."

"No, we'll soon dig him out," said Daddy Martin. "The rest of you stay here. Ruth," he went on to his wife, "get some hot water ready, and a bed. If that poor boy has been snowed up in that bungalow for two or three days he must be almost dead, and half starved, too."

"But how did he get there?" asked Mrs. Martin.

"And who is he?" asked Aunt Jo.

"All I know is what I read in the note," replied the father of the Curlytops. "It may be the same lame boy who was in my store and ran away before I had a chance to talk to him."

"And maybe he's the one who you thought might have taken the pocketbook," added Uncle Frank.

"Well, we won't talk of that now," said Daddy Martin. "We'll get him dug out of the snow first, and ask him questions later. Come on!"

"How do you suppose Nicknack got to the bungalow?" asked Teddy.

"Oh, I guess he just dug his way through the snow, making a tunnel for himself from his barn," answered Mrs. Martin.

Whatever had happened to Nicknack he seemed glad now to be with his Curlytop friends. He ate the pieces of cookie and the cabbage leaves they gave him, and bleated to ask for more.

Turnover, the cat, and Skyrocket, the dog, who had been in the house ever since the big storm, were also glad to see their friend the goat.

"And we'll be glad to see that lame boy, whoever he is, when daddy and Uncle Frank dig him out," said Mother Martin.

With their big shovels it did not take the two men long to dig their way to the snow bungalow. The pile of white flakes was deep over it but not so deep that a tunnel had to be cut, though it was through a tunnel, as they found out afterward, that Nicknack had made his way from the bungalow to the house. Only it was a small tunnel, such as an animal would make wallowing his way through the drifts.

The day before, when looking for Nicknack, Uncle Frank and Daddy Martin had tunneled to the bungalow door, but in the night this tunnel had caved in, so they had to do the work over again.

"Here we are!" cried Uncle Frank, as his shovel struck on some wood. "This is the bungalow. Now to see who's inside of it!"

"Here's the place where the goat got out," went on Mr. Martin. "Whoever tied that note on his neck must have pulled loose a board to let him get out into the snow. Hello in there!" he called, striking with his shovel on the bungalow.

"Yes—I'm here," came back the faint answer.

"We'll have you out in a few minutes," cheerfully called Daddy Martin. "You'll soon be all right!"

Then he and Uncle Frank made larger the hole where the board had been torn off, for the snow was piled up against the door, having drifted heavily during the night.

As they entered the bungalow, after knocking off more boards, they saw, lying on the rug and a piece of carpet in the corner, a boy who, when he tried to stand up, almost fell.

"I—I'm sorry," he began, "but I——"

"Now don't say another word!" exclaimed Daddy Martin. "We'll take you to the house and you can talk afterward—after you've had something to eat and when you get warm. You'll be all right! Don't worry!"

Picking the boy up in his arms Mr. Martin carried him through the snow to the warm house. There the Curlytops and others gathered about him.

"He isn't Hal," whispered Janet after a look.

"No," answered her brother. "That isn't Hal."

"But he's lame," went on Janet, as she saw the boy limping across the room to a chair near the fire which Mrs. Martin made comfortable for him with blankets. "He's lame a whole lot!"

The Curlytops were anxious to hear the boy's story, but Daddy Martin would not let him talk until he had eaten some food and taken some warm milk.

"Now we'll listen to you," said Uncle Frank. "How did you come to go into the bungalow?"

"I went in there to get out of the storm," answered the boy. "My name is Arthur Wharton, and I used to be in the same Crippled Children's Home with Hal Chester. That's how I knew your name and where you lived. Hal told me. And when I was taken out of the Home I came to Cresco to find you, for I thought maybe you would help me," and he looked at Daddy Martin.

"Who took you away from the Home?" asked the Curlytops' father.

"A man who had charge of me after my father and mother died. They put me in the Home to get cured, but when they died this man, who had charge of what money my father left, said there was not enough to keep me there with the other boys and girls.

"So he took me out and made me go to work. Only I couldn't do much on account of my lame foot. So I ran away from that man. I had a little money saved up, and I came here. I heard Hal say how kind the Curlytops were and I wanted to see if their father could help me."

"Did you once come to my store?" asked Mr. Martin.

"Yes, I did," answered the lame boy. Mr. Martin did not speak of the lost pocketbook and money.

"Why didn't you wait to see me?" asked Ted's father.

"Because, after I was sitting in your store waiting for you, I got to thinking and I got scared for fear you'd send me back to that bad man who used me so hard. So I went out when the clerk wasn't looking. I got another place to work, and made enough to live on, but it was not as nice as when my father and mother were alive."

"And did you afterward come to this house and ring the bell?" asked Mrs. Martin.

"Yes, I was going to ask you to help me. But, at the last minute, I got afraid again and ran away. After that I didn't know what to do. I got a little work, but it wasn't much, and three or four days ago I was discharged because I was too slow on account of my lame foot. I worked in a store over at Butler." This was a place about five miles from Cresco.

"I thought maybe I could get work in your store," went on Arthur to Mr. Martin, "so I started to walk here again from Butler. I wasn't going to run away from you this time. But the storm came up, I lost my way and in the dark I crawled into the snow-covered house back of yours. First I thought it was a part of the stable. I found some things to eat in it."

"We left them from our play party," said Teddy.

"I'm glad you did," went on the lame boy with a smile, "for that is all I had. Then my foot got worse when it began to storm. Then I saw I was snowed in and I knew I'd have to stay. But I got hungry and I had only a crust of bread left, for I ate all the rest of your things, and I had to let snow melt in my hand and drink the water. Then the goat came in. I knew he was your goat, 'cause Hal had told me about Nicknack. The goat stayed with me all last night, and I snuggled up to him and kept warm. Then I thought maybe I could send him for help. I'd read of men in the mountains doing that with the dogs.

"I had a pencil, a paper and some string in my pocket. So I wrote a note and tied it on the goat's neck. Then I tore loose a board in the side of the little house and the goat began to burrow out through the snow. The hole he came in by was snowed shut. Then I guess I must have gone to sleep for that's all I remember until I heard you calling to me just now."

"Well, you have had a hard time," said Mr. Martin, "but now we will take care of you. Don't worry any more."

And Arthur did not. After a good meal to make him forget his hunger, he was put in a warm bed, and the next day he was much better. The storm was over now, and people were beginning to dig themselves out after having been snowed in for so long a time.

One of Mr. Martin's clerks came up from the store to say that everything was all right down there, and he brought other good news.

"That pocketbook we thought the lame boy took," he said, "has been found."

"Where?" asked Mr. Martin, eagerly.

"It had fallen under a box and I saw it there when I cleaned the store and moved the box," was the answer.

"Oh, I'm so glad!" cried Teddy, when he heard the news.

"So'm I!" added Janet

They did not tell Arthur that, at one time, it was thought he might have taken the money. They did not want to make him feel bad. For he was happy now, with the Curlytops.

"Can he always live with us?" asked Janet.

"I like him," added Ted.

"I'm glad you do," said their father. "But I think it will be best to send him back to the Home for a while, as a doctor told me he could be cured of his lameness if he stayed about a year. So we'll send Arthur back and in the summer we can go to see him when we visit at Cherry Farm."

Arthur said he would be glad to go back to the Home, for he had many friends there and liked it, though he liked the Curlytops, too. The man who was his guardian tried to make trouble and keep the boy from going back to be cured, but Mr. Martin and Uncle Frank soon had matters straightened out, and another guardian was put in charge of Arthur.

When the big storm was over the Curlytops had more fun on their skates and sleds. Then they got ready for Christmas. Arthur stayed with them until after the holidays. Then, much better than when he ran away and went wandering about in the cold, he was sent back to the Home, where, a year later, he was cured so he did not limp any more.

"And if it hadn't been that Nicknack found him in the bungalow and brought the note to us through the snow, we might not have known until too late that Arthur was there," said Mother Martin.

"Nicknack is a good goat!" exclaimed Teddy. "We'll always take him with us."

"Are you going to bring him out to the ranch when you come to see me?" asked Uncle Frank.

"Are we going out to your ranch?" asked Janet.

"Yes. I have spoken to your father about it, and he says you may come. But not until winter is over. It is no fun out there when it is cold."

What the children did when they went out to Montana you may learn by reading the next book of this series to be called: "The Curlytops at Uncle Frank's Ranch; or, Little Folks on Ponyback."

"Well, we had lots of fun being snowed in, didn't we?" asked Janet of her brother, after New Year's Day, when Arthur had said good-bye and gone back to the Home.

"Oh, we had an awful good time!" cried Teddy. "The best ever!"

Then Teddy and Janet went skating and had fun, with plenty more in prospect when they should go out West to Uncle Frank's ranch.

THE END

THE CURLYTOPS SERIES

By HOWARD R. GARIS

12mo. Cloth. Illustrated. Jacket in full colors Price per volume, 50 cents. Postage 10 cents additional.

1. THE CURLYTOPS AT CHERRY FARM
or Vacation Days in the Country

A tale of happy vacation days on a farm.

2. THE CURLYTOPS ON STAR ISLAND
or Camping Out with Grandpa

The Curlytops camp on Star Island.

3. THE CURLYTOPS SNOWED IN
or Grand Fun with Skates and Sleds

The Curlytops on lakes and hills.

4. THE CURLYTOPS AT UNCLE FRANK'S RANCH
or Little Folks on Ponyback

Out West on their uncle's ranch they have a wonderful time.

5. THE CURLYTOPS AT SILVER LAKE
or On the Water with Uncle Ben

The Curlytops camp out on the shores of a beautiful lake.

6. THE CURLYTOPS AND THEIR PETS
or Uncle Toby's Strange Collection

An old uncle leaves them to care for his collection of pets.

7. THE CURLYTOPS AND THEIR PLAYMATES
or Jolly Times Through the Holidays

They have great times with their uncle's collection of animals.

8. THE CURLYTOPS IN THE WOODS
or Fun at the Lumber Camp

Exciting times in the forest for Curlytops.

9. THE CURLYTOPS AT SUNSET BEACH
or What Was Found in the Sand

The Curlytops have a fine time at the seashore.

10. THE CURLYTOPS TOURING AROUND
or The Missing Photograph Albums

The Curlytops get in some moving pictures.

11. THE CURLYTOPS IN A SUMMER CAMP
or Animal Joe's Menagerie

There is great excitement as some mischievous monkeys break out of Animal Joe's Menagerie.

12. THE CURLYTOPS GROWING UP
or Winter Sports and Summer Pleasures

Little Trouble is a host in himself and his larger brother and sister are never still a minute, but go from one little adventure to another in a way to charm all youthful readers.

Send for Our Free Illustrated Catalogue.

CUPPLES & LEON COMPANY, PublishersNew York

THE RUTH FIELDING SERIES

By ALICE B. EMERSON

12mo. Illustrated. Jacket in full colors.

Price 50 cents per volume.
Postage 10 cents additional.

Ruth Fielding was an orphan and came to live with her miserly uncle. Her adventures and travels make stories that will hold the interest of every reader.

Ruth Fielding is a character that will live in juvenile fiction.

1. RUTH FIELDING OF THE RED MILL
2. RUTH FIELDING AT BRIARWOOD HALL
3. RUTH FIELDING AT SNOW CAMP
4. RUTH FIELDING AT LIGHTHOUSE POINT
5. RUTH FIELDING AT SILVER RANCH
6. RUTH FIELDING ON CLIFF ISLAND
7. RUTH FIELDING AT SUNRISE FARM
8. RUTH FIELDING AND THE GYPSIES
9. RUTH FIELDING IN MOVING PICTURES

10. RUTH FIELDING DOWN IN DIXIE
11. RUTH FIELDING AT COLLEGE
12. RUTH FIELDING IN THE SADDLE
13. RUTH FIELDING IN THE RED CROSS
14. RUTH FIELDING AT THE WAR FRONT
15. RUTH FIELDING HOMEWARD BOUND
16. RUTH FIELDING DOWN EAST
17. RUTH FIELDING IN THE GREAT NORTHWEST
18. RUTH FIELDING ON THE ST. LAWRENCE
19. RUTH FIELDING TREASURE HUNTING
20. RUTH FIELDING IN THE FAR NORTH
21. RUTH FIELDING AT GOLDEN PASS
22. RUTII FIELDING IN ALASKA
23. RUTH FIELDING AND HER GREAT SCENARIO
24. RUTH FIELDING AT CAMERON HALL
25. RUTH FIELDING CLEARING HER NAME

CUPPLES & LEON COMPANY, PublishersNew York

CPSIA information can be obtained
at www.ICGtesting.com
Printed in the USA
LVHW022357210621
690829LV00006B/210